A runaway cousin . . .

"Aunt Laura," Elizabeth said. "Have you seen Kelly?"

"Kelly?" Aunt Laura wrinkled her brow. "Isn't she with you?"

"Well, um . . ." Elizabeth licked her lips. "She sort of disappeared. We thought she might have come downstairs."

Aunt Laura blinked. She swung around to Mrs. Wakefield. "What's going on, Alice?" she asked, a note of worry in her voice. "You haven't seen my daughter, have you?"

Mrs. Wakefield shook her head. "What time was this, girls?"

"Um, maybe half an hour ago?" Jessica guessed.

"Where could she be?" Aunt Laura's eyes opened very wide. Mrs. Wakefield put a restraining hand on her sister's shoulder. "Do you mean that Kelly's lost?"

Visit the Official Sweet Valley Web Site on the Internet at:

http://www.sweetvalley.com

SWEET VALLEY TWINS

Sisters at War

Written by
Jamie Suzanne

Created by
FRANCINE PASCAL

BANTAM BOOKS
NEW YORK • TORONTO • LONDON • SYDNEY • AUCKLAND

To Kacey Michelle Cotton

RL 4, 008-012

SISTERS AT WAR
A Bantam Book / November 1997

*Sweet Valley High® and Sweet Valley Twins® are
registered trademarks of Francine Pascal.*

Conceived by Francine Pascal.

*Produced by Daniel Weiss Associates, Inc.
33 West 17th Street
New York, NY 10011.*

Cover art by Bruce Emmett.

ISBN: 0-553-48442-7

Published simultaneously in the United States and Canada

*Bantam Books are published by Bantam Books, a division of Bantam
Doubleday Dell Publishing Group, Inc. Its trademark, consisting of the
words "Bantam Books" and the portrayal of a rooster, is Registered in the
U.S. Patent and Trademark Office and in other countries. Marca
Registrada. Bantam Books, 1540 Broadway, New York, New York 10036.*

PRINTED IN THE UNITED STATES OF AMERICA

OPM   0 9 8 7 6 5 4 3 2 1

One

◇

Jessica Wakefield woke up to the sound of banging. *Who could be making that awful racket?* Jessica thought as she turned over in her bed. *Am I the only person who realizes that today is a holiday, and holidays are for sleeping late?* The banging didn't stop.

Jessica sat up, then plopped down again. She pulled her pillow over her ears. "Mmmph!" she said.

Her twin sister's voice came from beyond Jessica's door. "It's Elizabeth, Jess, can I come in?"

Jessica opened one eye. "No," she responded, putting on her best grumpy voice.

Elizabeth laughed and walked in. She sat down on her twin's bed. "Come on, Jessica, we have a lot of planning to do. Today's the day!"

Suddenly, Jessica pulled the pillow off her head. "Oh my gosh!" she said. "You're right!" She and Elizabeth looked at each other and said in unison, "The cousins are coming!"

It was the day before Thanksgiving, and the Wakefields were hosting dinner this year. That meant that Mrs. Wakefield's sisters were coming for a visit and bringing their daughters. Aunt Nancy had two girls, Robin and Stacey. Aunt Laura had Kelly. Although Stacey was only eight years old, both Robin and Kelly were the same age as the twins. And although the twins had seen Robin fairly recently, Kelly had moved with Aunt Laura to Tucson four years ago, and this was her first visit back to Sweet Valley.

"I can't wait to see them!" exclaimed Elizabeth. "Remember how much Kelly looks like us?"

"Yes," said Jessica, concentrating, "well, sort of. We haven't seen her in a while. I wonder whether she still looks the same."

"Well . . . ," Elizabeth teased her sister, "I bet she'll be taller."

Jessica laughed at that, and Elizabeth smiled. Elizabeth added, "I hope she hasn't changed that much. She was always so much fun when we were kids—remember the Door Mouse?" Was Elizabeth kidding? Of course Jessica remembered! When the twins and Kelly were little and Kelly had lived in Sweet Valley, they had loved to act out scenes from *Alice's Adventures in Wonderland*. Jessica's favorite had always been the tea party scene. Jessica would dress up outrageously as the Mad Hatter, Elizabeth would do her best innocent Alice, and Kelly did a hysterical impersonation of the sleepy, space-cadet Dormouse.

"And Robin's *always* a blast," said Jessica. Robin was the twins' favorite cousin, but that was because they knew her the best. Robin was only a few months younger than the twins, and the three girls loved hanging out together. Robin's dad, the twins' Uncle Kirk, often called them "The Three Musketeers." Once, when Robin had come for a visit, she'd developed a huge crush on Todd Wilkins, Elizabeth's sort-of boyfriend, but that was before she knew that Todd liked Elizabeth. They had gotten everything sorted out, and their friendship was stronger than ever.

"Yeah," Elizabeth agreed. "She's terrific."

"So, what fun events do we have planned?" Jessica asked her sister.

Right at that moment, there was a knock at the door.

"Come in," Elizabeth called out.

"Unless it's Steven," added Jessica.

Their mother poked her head in the door. "Girls, I need you to get dressed and ready." Jessica shifted on the bed as her mother eyed her pajamas. "We have some work to do today."

"What kind of work?" asked Elizabeth.

"We need to clean the house," replied her mother. "I want everything to be perfect by the time my sisters arrive."

"No problem, Mom," Elizabeth said. "We'll be glad to help, right, Jessica?"

"Actually . . . ," Jessica hedged, "I sort of told Lila—"

"Well, un-tell her," Mrs. Wakefield said. "I need your help, and that's final. I want to see you girls downstairs in twenty minutes. Chop, chop." And she turned and left the room.

Jessica raised her eyebrows. It was unlike her mother to act like such a drill sergeant. *Looks like we're in for some big fun today,* she thought.

As if she were reading her mind, Elizabeth said, "Looks like Mom is in a pretty bad mood."

"Oh, well," Jessica sighed. "How long can a little cleaning take?"

"Now what, Mom?" Jessica asked, wearily replacing the mop in the broom closet and hanging the bucket on its hook. She had just mopped the kitchen floor and hoped that this would be the last chore of the morning.

Deep down, however, she guessed that it probably wasn't.

"Let's see." Mrs. Wakefield hunched over a checklist, and Jessica peered over her shoulder. To her dismay, she saw that her mother's list covered two whole pages—and it was in small type. *She typed the to-do list?* "Fresh cranberry sauce . . . I guess we can leave that one till tomorrow. Mopping the floors . . . check." Mrs. Wakefield crossed off that task with a large red slash. "Ah! The pumpkin tarts!"

"The what?" Jessica asked suspiciously. Jessica was beginning to wish that she didn't have this vacation day from school. As she slogged her way through one chore after another, she was having fantasies about being in the school cafeteria. Or in homeroom. Or even in science class. Somewhere she'd be *safe.* "I can't make pumpkin tarts," she pointed out.

Mrs. Wakefield shook her head. "Don't worry, I'll make them. I thought it would be nice if everyone had a little pumpkin tart for dessert. The perfect ending to a lovely old-fashioned Thanksgiving dinner, don't you think? Especially with all the relatives coming."

"Yeah," Jessica agreed, "but . . ." *It seems like an awful lot of work,* she told herself, wrinkling her nose. "Wouldn't it make more sense to just buy them?"

"Buy them?" Mrs. Wakefield stared curiously at Jessica. "No, honey, I want this Thanksgiving to be just perfect, and store-bought pumpkin tarts are not . . . appropriate."

"But . . . ," Jessica tried again. It wasn't that she was sick of cleaning and doing things for the holiday, exactly—well, OK, she *was* sick of cleaning—but it was also that Thanksgiving was supposed to be restful and peaceful, and it hadn't been restful so far today at all. Not even close. "Pumpkin tarts are hard to make, aren't they? Wouldn't it be easier to bake a couple of pumpkin pies?" *And use the time we save to do something fun, like plan what we're going to do when Robin and Kelly get here?*

It was too bad that Jessica's sort-of boyfriend, Aaron Dallas, wouldn't be around. He and his family were away on a ski trip over the break, so she wouldn't be seeing him till Monday. *Monday.* Jessica sighed. Monday seemed such a long way off. She wished she were skiing with Aaron instead of cooped up here cleaning this hopelessly clean house. Mrs. Wakefield shook her head. "Anybody can make a pumpkin pie. Tarts are my specialty. Don't you think the family is worth it?"

Jessica decided she'd better not answer that question. "Aunt Nancy never goes to all this trouble when we visit her."

"All the more reason we should do things right when they come visit us." Mrs. Wakefield returned to her list. "Have you cleaned your room yet?"

Jessica nodded. Actually, she'd hung up her jacket and shoved everything else under the bed, but her mother didn't need to know that. "Totally clean," she promised, crossing her fingers behind her back.

Elizabeth came into the kitchen and dropped a dust cloth on the table. "Done," she said, sighing heavily. "But I don't understand why I had to dust all the lightbulbs in the dining room—"

"Because it has to be perfect," Mrs. Wakefield interrupted. "And that means paying attention to the details."

"If I had to mop the floors and even clean the front of the dishwasher, Elizabeth," Jessica groaned, "then you shouldn't complain about a little dusting. Dusting's *way* easier than what I just did."

Her twin frowned. "At least people *see* the front of the dishwasher," she pointed out. "People don't see lightbulbs."

"Nobody would have been able to see the tiny spot I found. It was the only one on the whole dishwasher," Jessica said, feeling virtuous. "But I noticed it, and I cleaned it."

Elizabeth shrugged. "If it was so tiny, then it

doesn't sound like wiping it off was so hard," she said sensibly.

Jessica sighed and rolled her eyes. *Sisters.* Though she and Elizabeth looked exactly alike, with long blond hair and bluish green eyes, they were really very different. Jessica lived for parties, fashion, and large groups of kids, and she never minded a few pizza crusts scattered around the carpet or a bed that got made once a month or so. Elizabeth, on the other hand, preferred reading, writing, and spending time with a couple of especially close friends, and she cheerfully described herself as a clean freak who liked to have everything in its place. Despite their differences, however, the two girls were usually the best of friends.

Elizabeth took an apple from the fruit basket on the countertop. "Mom, are we ready for a break? There's this movie I really, really want to rent for Robin."

"What movie?" Jessica asked curiously.

"The new Eileen Thomas film," Elizabeth explained. *"View from the Hotel Windermere.* My English teacher recommended it, and—"

"Oh, spare me," Jessica groaned. *View from the Hotel Whatever* sounded right up Elizabeth's alley. She could picture it now: talky and meaningful, with English accents, weird costumes, and lots of people looking depressed. "Robin doesn't like movies like *that*. Robin likes *good* movies. I bet she hasn't seen *Too Cool for High School*. Let's rent that instead."

"*Too Cool for High School*?" Elizabeth's eyes widened. "But we've already seen that! Anyway, Robin *does* want to see *View from the Hotel Windermere*. She wrote me and said how much she loved Eileen Thomas."

Jessica flipped her hair. "The reason we've already seen *Too Cool* is because it's an awesome movie."

"Come on, Jess. You always get to pick the movie." Elizabeth looked hurt.

"That is utterly false. What about last week when you made me watch that movie about the ice-skater with the crippling disease?"

"That was last *June!*" shrieked Elizabeth. "Besides, you said you *wanted* to watch it!"

"I never said I wanted to watch that stupid movie!"

Mrs. Wakefield held up her hand. "Don't fight, girls."

"Fine!" Elizabeth snapped. "Rent *Too Cool for High School*! Just watch it on a night when Robin and I are going out. And don't plan to use the VCR tonight because Robin and I—"

Jessica clenched her fists. She knew that it didn't make much sense, but for some reason she was furious with her twin. Maybe it was just because Jessica was exhausted after all of the cleaning, but somehow letting Elizabeth get her way seemed like more than she could bear at that moment. "Robin wrote me too," she lied, "and she said she's dying to see *Too Cool*."

"Girls, stop it right now." Mrs. Wakefield's voice was firm. "No fighting. We have far too much to do." She glanced at the list. "Jessica, unload the dishwasher. Elizabeth, scour the sink. And if you two can't get along—" The sentence hung in the air, unfinished, but Jessica had no doubt that her mother meant business.

Jessica flung open the dishwasher door with a bang. "It's not *my* fault," she began. "If *Elizabeth* would only—"

"*I* didn't do anything," Elizabeth said innocently.

"Girls!"

Jessica sighed and grabbed three plastic mugs from the top rack of the machine.

It wasn't that she *liked* arguing with her sister. It was just that . . . that sometimes it was impossible not to.

Elizabeth bent low over the sink, scrubbing hard. Behind her she could hear her sister shoving knives and forks into the silverware drawer. She sighed. Much as she loved Jessica, sometimes her twin was difficult to deal with. So Elizabeth wanted to watch a movie with Robin. What was so wrong with that?

"Where is everyone going to sleep?" she asked her mother.

"Stacey and Robin will share the pullout couch in the living room," her mother explained. "And, Elizabeth, you'll need to move your stuff into Jessica's room so that Aunt Nancy and Uncle Kirk can have yours."

Elizabeth's jaw dropped. "*I* have to share with *Jessica?*" she asked indignantly. She hadn't meant to sound so obnoxious, but really, the floor in her sister's room was totally covered with junk.

"Watch your tone, Elizabeth. I think you can live with your sister for a couple of days," Mrs. Wakefield said.

"Oh, Mom," she groaned. But Elizabeth knew when she was beaten. Swallowing hard, she swung back to the sink and turned on the hot water full force.

Great. Just great.

Now Elizabeth had to share a room with the person who was driving her crazy!

"But I still don't get it, Mom," Jessica said crossly later that morning. She'd finished unloading the dishwasher and was now lazily running a sponge across the glass table in the living room, trying to make the job last as long as possible so that she wouldn't have to move on to the next one. Visions of Aaron Dallas filled her brain. She wished he weren't on vacation. Aaron would definitely want to watch *Too Cool for High School* with her. But no, she had to spend *her* vacation doing her Cinderella impersonation so that her mother could win the Housekeeper of the Year award. She sighed. "Why does the house have to be so perfect? Nobody's *perfect*."

Mrs. Wakefield barely looked up from her list. Jessica had a sudden urge to grab it and . . . and bury it, or burn it, or toss it in the Pacific Ocean, or something. "You're right, nobody's perfect," Mrs. Wakefield agreed. "So I'll rephrase that: The house doesn't have to be perfect—just as good as we can make it."

"But why?" Jessica pressed. Her mother was a tidy person, but not usually *this* tidy. It was like aliens from the planet Clean had taken over her brain or something. "Aunt Nancy's house isn't like this. And I've never visited Aunt Laura in Arizona, but when she used to live in Sweet Valley, her entire house was way worse than my room."

Mrs. Wakefield didn't crack a smile. "Nothing could possibly be worse than your room. Sometimes I think we need to tack up a Condemned sign on the door. Anyway, there were other reasons why Aunt Laura's house wasn't clean. Reasons that didn't have a lot to do with her."

"You mean Uncle Greg?" Jessica asked curiously. "I mean, ex–Uncle Greg?" Greg Bates, Aunt Laura's former husband, was a totally funny guy. He was very handsome and charming, and Jessica had always liked him a lot, even though she knew he was kind of irresponsible.

Mrs. Wakefield looked pensive. "That's right," she admitted. "He never, ever helped with the housework. Poor Laura had to do everything herself, even though she had a full-time job. Not that he really could have helped; he was never home much."

"That's so sad," Jessica said with feeling. It always made her feel grown-up when her mother discussed private details of her relatives' lives with her.

Mrs. Wakefield shuddered. "Oh, honey, it was very sad," she said. "Greg loved Laura a lot, and she loved him, but he was utterly undependable. He wasn't ready to be a good father and husband. Of course, Kelly adores him, and Laura will never say a word against him, but I never really trusted Greg Bates. I always told Laura she would have been better off with—" She paused.

"With what?" Jessica wanted to know, trying to keep the exasperation out of her voice. Her mother had no business starting to tell her all these juicy and exciting details, then backing away. "She would have been better off with what, Mom?"

Mrs. Wakefield smiled broadly. "Never mind," she replied. "But don't be surprised if something very interesting happens over the weekend."

"Huh?" Jessica hated it when grown-ups spoke in riddles. "You mean, like, Uncle Greg is coming?"

"Not a chance." The smile faded from Mrs. Wakefield's face. "Have you finished cleaning already?" she asked pointedly. "Don't forget the spot in the center of the table." Turning, she left the room.

Jessica sighed and sprayed a little more cleanser on the sponge.

Mom is definitely acting like an alien, she thought.

"Okay, Mom, I fixed the wobbly desk in the den," Jessica said. "What's my next assignment?" Jessica was hoping against hope that her mother would tell her to take a break.

"Wonderful, sweetie! Would you please make up the foldout couch in there so that Laura and Kelly can use it as a bed?" Her mother busily scanned her list.

"No problem, Mom." *It's easier to just agree,* thought Jessica, *and act cheerful. Besides, that's the kind of chore that could take a really long time, if I do it right.*

Jessica was in the den, pondering whether or not to flip on the television set and catch the last of *The Phyllis Hartley Show,* when Elizabeth burst in.

"Hey, Jess, how's the cleaning going?"

"Oh, fine. I have to make up this foldout couch. Want to help?"

"Sure." Elizabeth smiled and grabbed an end of the sheet. The twins shook it, and it billowed out. In fact, Elizabeth's side flew right out of her hand and fluttered to the floor. As Elizabeth reached out to grab the end of the sheet, Jessica saw her glance at something. Elizabeth's head shot up.

"What's that?" Elizabeth asked, pointing down.

"What?" Jessica responded.

"That. Under the leg of the desk?" Elizabeth's voice was a little impatient.

"Oh. That. That is what I used to fix the desk. It was wobbly, so I just shoved that book under the leg. Pretty smart, eh?" Jessica tapped her forehead with her index finger.

"Jessica," Elizabeth said with a sigh, "that is my new book on rock and mineral collecting."

"Oh!" Jessica exclaimed. "Well, it's the perfect size to go under the desk leg and prop it up. You can have it back on Sunday, when everybody leaves. OK? Now let's make this bed!"

"Jessica!" Elizabeth's eyes were huge. "I had to

save up a lot of money to buy that book! I bought it with my allowance! And now it's getting a big dent right in the middle of it!"

"Well, I'm sorry, Lizzie. If I had known it was so important to you, I would have used another book." Jessica gave a little pout and played with the ends of her long blond hair. "But what's the big deal? Are there any burning secrets about rocks and minerals that can't wait a few days for you to uncover them?"

"That's not the point and you know it!" Elizabeth said. She seemed to be getting more and more impatient.

Jessica rolled her eyes. Really, this rock and mineral collecting hobby of Elizabeth's was too dorky for her to deal with. And she certainly didn't want to waste time arguing about it. "Fine. I'll take the stupid book out from under the desk, OK? Happy now?" Jessica reached down and removed the book. The desk immediately tipped ever so slightly in the direction of the shorter leg.

"It has a dent in it," Elizabeth said.

For goodness sake, what does she want me to do? Jessica thought as she grabbed the book. She opened the front cover and gave it a whack from the inside in order to remove the dent. Unfortunately, that only caused a bigger dent, one going in the opposite direction. "Um. Oops!" Jessica said.

Elizabeth grabbed the book. "Forget it. Please don't help me. You've done enough." She turned to stalk out of the room.

"Elizabeth! You know I didn't do that on purpose," Jessica pleaded.

Elizabeth stopped and sighed. Then she turned back around. "I know you didn't. But, Jessica, I don't want you taking my things without asking. OK?"

Jessica knew that she was wrong, but the way Elizabeth was talking to her made her feel like she was three years old. "Of course that's OK!" she snapped. Elizabeth's eyebrows shot up. She looked like she was about to cry. *That didn't sound very nice,* Jessica said to herself. "I'm sorry, I didn't mean that the way it sounded. I do understand, and I'm sorry I took your book without asking."

Elizabeth smiled and shook her head. "Apology accepted." She put the book down. "Now I think we have a bed to make!"

Two

◇

"This is your sweater, you know," Jessica said happily, dropping a light blue cardigan on the steps at Elizabeth's feet. "*You* take it upstairs." Jessica was thrilled. It was hard to catch her sister being a slob; this was a golden opportunity for teasing.

Holding the vacuum hose steady, Elizabeth took the sweater. "Well, you could be a little nicer about it," she reminded her sister. She straightened up slowly. Her back ached, and it was only just after lunchtime. This day was taking forever.

Jessica's only response was a shrug.

"Wait a minute." Elizabeth turned the sweater around in her hands. She didn't really mind taking the sweater up to her room—it would be a change from vacuuming the stairs at least—but something occurred to her. She turned off the vacuum. "Where'd you find this anyway?" she asked.

"Shoved behind the couch pillows." Jessica sighed deeply, as if putting up with a messy sister like Elizabeth was more than she could bear.

Elizabeth frowned. "Hold on, Jess. This *is* my sweater—"

"Didn't we already have this conversation?" Jessica interrupted.

Elizabeth tried to put on her brightest smile. "But *you* were the last one to wear it. You borrowed it that Friday when you and Lila went to the—"

Jessica waved her hand in the air. "Oh, I did not either."

"But you *did*," Elizabeth insisted. "I distinctly remember you coming into my room and asking if I had anything to wear, and when you saw my sweater you said, 'Oh, that's really cool!'"

Jessica snorted. "No, I didn't," she said, but she didn't sound as sure anymore.

"You did too!" Elizabeth's eyes blazed. "Those were your exact words! And then you took it off and put it somewhere."

"You're making that up." A flash of discomfort crossed Jessica's face.

"And when I asked you about the sweater, you

just shrugged and said, 'That old thing? It's around somewhere.'" Elizabeth set her jaw. "Which is fairly typical."

"No way," Jessica objected. "*If* I borrowed your sweater, which I'm not saying I did, I returned it. Like I *always* do."

"Are you *kidding?*" Elizabeth nearly shouted. She was usually very patient with Jessica, but after a day of cleaning, she was tired and cranky. "You never return *anything!*"

"Jessica and Elizabeth!" shouted Mrs. Wakefield from the other room. "I want to hear less arguing and more cleaning! If neither of you has enough to do, you can come down here and help me iron the dish towels!"

Elizabeth and Jessica started at each other in horror. "*Iron* the dish towels?" Elizabeth whispered. "Is she kidding?"

"I think our mother has lost her mind," Jessica said. Elizabeth nodded, finally in agreement with her sister about something.

"So where are Aunt Laura and Kelly going to sleep?" Elizabeth asked her mother. There was less than an hour to go before the visitors would start to arrive, and she was sitting at the kitchen counter helping her mother polish the silver.

"In the den," Mrs. Wakefield explained, glancing quickly at the clock. "Only forty-five minutes and so much to be done. . . ." She sighed. "I sent Jessica to make up the bed for them."

Elizabeth hid her smile. She and her sister had finished making the bed twenty minutes ago. Jessica had the incredible ability to stretch the length of any chore into infinity.

"No one's taking *my* room, I hope," Steven remarked, bursting into the kitchen. He set down a large paper bag, then flung open the refrigerator and reached for the milk. "If some twerp cousin of mine wants it, she can arm wrestle me for it. And may the best *man* win."

"Careful with the milk, Steven," Mrs. Wakefield told him. "Don't drink straight out of the carton like a caveman. Use a glass. We have company coming."

"I know, I know," Steven grumbled. He yanked open the cabinet and grabbed a coffee mug. "But it'll just take energy to wash this, you know," he complained, pouring milk into the cup till it overflowed. "Bad for the environment and—"

"Steven!" Mrs. Wakefield barked. "Get a cloth and wipe it up."

"OK, OK," Steven said, putting his hands up in mock surrender. "Just let me take a swig of this first." He lifted the mug to his lips. Elizabeth wasn't entirely surprised when more milk splashed onto the counter.

"Steven!" Mrs. Wakefield snapped. "I told you to clean up the spill, not create more of a mess. Besides, you need to put the milk away, close the refrigerator, and—"

"Well, don't go postal on me," Steven muttered. "Which do you want me to do first? Like, I only have two hands." He set the mug down with a thump. More milk sloshed over the brim of the cup and trickled down the side. "The trouble with you, Mom, is that you get all bent out of shape every time you go on a cleaning binge. No offense or anything, but you've got to learn to live with a little mess. A little ambiguity, like my English teacher keeps saying." He clapped his hand to his forehead before Mrs. Wakefield could speak. "Oh! Speaking of English teachers, I've got this project I need your help with, Mom."

"Speaking of projects, Steven," Mrs. Wakefield said, "I asked you to clean the bathrooms. Did you?"

"Well, not exactly," Steven admitted cheerfully. "But that's because you sent me to the store instead. Like, four times. Anyway, this is a really, really interesting project. It's all about—"

"I only sent you to the store three times," Mrs. Wakefield reminded him.

"What's the project about?" Elizabeth asked curiously. If she could get Steven talking about it, she reasoned, maybe her mother would get interested in it too, and they'd be able to skip the rest of the polishing. Quietly, she set down the fork she was holding.

"Four times," Steven insisted. He turned to Elizabeth. "Did you hear about the last one? Mom sent me to the store for sardines or fried octopus or whatever it is that you put into Caesar salad—"

"I certainly hope you got the *anchovies*," Mrs. Wakefield broke in, rifling through the shopping bag. Elizabeth thought she caught a glimmer of a smile at the corner of her mother's mouth.

". . . and then she thinks of something else she needs too," Steven went on. "So what does she do? Send you out, or Jessica? Or drive herself? No *way*." He shook his head. "So there I am, in the store, waiting in line already with my sliced shark scales and, oh yeah, the two hunks of lettuce she remembered as I was heading out the driveway, and suddenly there's, like, this disembodied voice coming over the loudspeaker, and it's saying, 'Steven Wakefield, paging Mr. Steven Wakefield.'" Steven pretended to speak into a microphone.

"Steven," Mrs. Wakefield said as she pulled out two huge heads of lettuce from the bag. "I distinctly remember telling you *leaf* lettuce—"

"Hey, it has leaves, doesn't it?" Steven retorted. "So my stomach, like, practically falls out of my *body*, know what I mean?" he asked, turning back to Elizabeth. "And I'm standing there thinking, What terrible thing's happened? Did Dad get murdered? Did something fall into Jessica's open mouth and choke her to death? Did Mom's cleaning binge send her over the edge? So I say, 'That's me!' and I run to the office, totally freaked out. And they hand me the phone, and it's Mom. So I'm, like, 'Mom! Is everything OK?' and my heart is pumping a hundred miles a minute"—Steven pretended to be terrified—"and she's, like, 'Green onions, Steven. I forgot to tell you to pick up green onions.'" He shook his head. "Talk about scaring a guy half to death! I have never been so embarrassed in my entire life."

By the end of Steven's story, even Mrs. Wakefield was laughing. "Oh my, I guess I have been going a bit overboard. But I haven't seen my sisters in a long time, and I want everything to be just right. I'm sorry if I've been driving you kids crazy, and I really want to thank you for your help." She turned to Steven. "And I'm sorry if you were worried."

"Oh, that's all right," Steven said grandly. "Just took thirty years off my life. But who wants to live to be a hundred and twenty-five anyway?"

Elizabeth cracked up. "So what's the project?"

"Family history," Steven said briefly. He picked up his cup and drank half the remaining milk. "A family tree plus a bunch of family stories. Due next Monday. I decided I'd better start now. Before the family all shows up. So how about it, Mom? I need names, dates, places. And *dirt*. Like, why did Aunt Laura marry that jerk Greg? And whatever happened to Grandma's cousin, the one who ran the so-called gas station that never sold any gas? And what was the dumbest argument you and your sisters ever had? Juicy stuff like that."

"First of all," Mrs. Wakefield said patiently, "please do not mention Greg Bates in front of Laura, all right? And second, my sisters and I had a perfect childhood. We were perfectly happy together. We never fought. We were happy to be sisters, and we were the best of friends." She shoved lettuce, anchovies, and onions into the refrigerator and straightened up with a sigh. "I suppose this lettuce will just have to do. There really isn't time to go back to the store. . . . "

"You *never* fought?" Somehow, Elizabeth had a hard time believing her mother. "I know you don't fight as adults, but you *must* have—"

"Never," Mrs. Wakefield insisted. "Just as I'm sure, Elizabeth, that you and your sister won't fight this weekend. We're one happy family, and I want everyone to know it."

"That'll be the day," Steven grumbled, dragging a wet rag through the milk on the counter-top.

"Happy families can fight too," Elizabeth argued. "I mean, Jess and I love each other. But sometimes we, like, get on each other's nerves."

Mrs. Wakefield frowned. "We *didn't* fight. Nancy, Laura, and I had a truly marvelous childhood. We all got along. I wish you kids got along as well."

"Me too," Steven complained. He tossed the rag into the sink. "Wakefield with the three-pointer! Of course, I'm practically perfect myself, so if it wasn't for this clown and that other kid who looks just like her . . ." He jerked his thumb at Elizabeth.

"Says you." Elizabeth made a face.

"Kids." Mrs. Wakefield held up a warning hand. "Please. I'm serious. This is a very important weekend to me for—for, well, for a lot of reasons. I want an old-fashioned family Thanksgiving, and so it's critical that you get along. And if you can't, fake it. Steven, I'll certainly help you with your project, but now's not a good time. Go clean the bathrooms, please. And, Elizabeth, keep polishing; I need to get started on the pumpkin tarts." She reached for a rolling pin. "Now where did I put that recipe?"

Elizabeth picked up the fork and rubbed it gently with silver polish.

She wondered how in the world her mother had managed to grow up with two sisters and never, ever argue with them.

Three

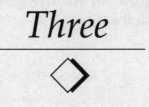

Steven sat at his desk in his bedroom, hunched over a spiral notebook. He looked nervously toward the door, hoping his mother wouldn't come up the stairs any time soon. She thought he was giving his room a last-second cleaning before the guests arrived, and he wasn't about to let her think otherwise.

With a black felt-tip marker he labeled the top of the first page "Wakefield Family Tree." He narrowed his eyes and stared at it. Then he shook his head. That didn't look quite right. *After all, not everybody in this family is a Wakefield*, he reminded himself. Carefully, he added the word "Steven" in front of his original heading. "The Steven Wakefield Family Tree," he muttered aloud, nodding. *Perfect.*

Was that a footfall on the steps? For a moment, Steven froze. Then he relaxed. No, he could definitely hear his mother's voice downstairs somewhere. Yelling at Jessica over the job she was doing, probably. He grinned to himself. "Steven Wakefield," he grunted as he wrote his name in big block capitals at the exact center of the paper. He was the most important member of the family, that was for sure. He considered adding a small "the Great" between his first and last names, since "Steven the Great Wakefield" had such a—well, such a *ring*—to it, but he decided not to. It wasn't his legal name, after all.

Not yet anyway.

Quickly, Steven wrote the names of his sisters next to his, only smaller of course, and connected them with a line. About an inch or so above their names, he sketched another line and wrote in the names of his parents. Then he added his aunts, uncles, and cousins. *Robin, Stacey, and Kelly,* he thought, sighing, as he tipped back in his chair. How come he hadn't been born into a family where there were *guys,* for crying out loud? He wished he had male cousins, cousins who played football and stuff, only not quite as well as he did, of course. Cousins with names like Kevin or Mike or, um, Frank. Names like that. But, oh no, that wasn't good enough for *his* family. No, he had to get stuck with a bunch of *girl* cousins. *Girls who giggle all the time and talk about makeup and—*

"What are you doing, Steven?"

Steven flung himself across his desk to hide the notebook, realizing as he did so that it was only Elizabeth. *And sneak up on a guy when he isn't looking,* he added mentally. "Nothing, nothing," he said.

"Are you sure?" Elizabeth put her hand on her hip.

Afraid that he looked ridiculous, Steven straightened up. "And what are *you* supposed to be doing?" he asked severely.

Elizabeth smiled. "Probably the same thing *you're* supposed to be doing," she said cheerfully. "What are you working on anyway?"

Steven wasn't quite sure what to say. Part of him wanted to keep his work private until he was done. On the other hand, maybe this would be a good opportunity to dazzle Elizabeth with all the stuff he knew about the family history. "Well . . ." He cleared his throat. "I mean, it's—"

"It's the family tree, isn't it?" Elizabeth took a step closer. "This is such a cool project. I wish I got to do something neat like this for homework."

"Someday, kiddo, someday." Steven sat back and dropped his marker casually on the desk. "When you're in high school like me." He made up his mind. With a quick motion of his hand, he spun the notebook so that it faced his sister. "I haven't gotten very far yet," he admitted, "with Field Marshal Mom downstairs and all, but I did get off to a pretty good start. What do you want to know?"

Elizabeth leaned over the desk. "Let's see . . . you've got Robin on there, right?" Her finger jabbed at Robin's name. "Yup, there she is. And there's Kelly. I think it's so cool the way there were four cousins all born in the same year: me, Jess, Kelly, and Robin."

I don't think it's so cool, Steven thought, but he didn't say so.

"Steven," Elizabeth began, "what do you know about Kelly?"

"What do you mean?" Steven snapped.

"Well—I mean . . . " Elizabeth hesitated. "What do you know about Greg Bates?"

Steven sighed. "I don't know that much, really. I know that he seemed like a nice, funny guy. But Mom sure never liked him very much. I think I've heard that he had a pretty bad temper, but I've never heard anything specific. He lives only a couple of towns away from here, but he travels to Europe a lot. The reason Aunt Laura never comes here for a visit is because she never wants to run into him again."

"How does Kelly feel about all of this?" Elizabeth asked, a look of worry on her face.

"How should I know? She probably misses her dad. Who wouldn't? My guess is that, as far as she's concerned, her dad is a funny, sweet man that her mother divorced."

"Doesn't Kelly ever see him?" Elizabeth frowned.

"Nope. One thing I can tell you for sure is that Greg Bates is a pretty unreliable guy. I don't think that spending quality time with Kelly is high on his list of priorities."

"It must be hard to have a dad like that," said Elizabeth.

"Yeah," Steven agreed. "It must."

"Hello?"

Jessica watched her mother scoop up the phone. With any luck, it would be the relatives saying they couldn't come. Then she could have her own room back, and maybe they could stop cleaning and just do fun things all weekend, like renting *Too Cool for High School* and watching it three or four times and sleeping late and going mall-hopping and . . .

"Oh, hi, Ned," Mrs. Wakefield said into the phone. "What's up?"

Ned. It was only her dad, probably calling from the airport where he'd gone to pick up Aunt Laura and Kelly. Jessica held her breath, half hoping the flight had been canceled. Maybe there was some humongous blizzard in Tucson. Did they have blizzards in Tucson?

"Oh, good," Mrs. Wakefield said, breaking into a smile. "For a moment I thought you were telling me the flight wasn't coming in! But it's on time?" She pressed the phone closer to her ear while Jessica sighed heavily.

"Oh . . . Yes . . . Uh-huh." Mrs. Wakefield's tone changed. Jessica looked up, curious, but her mother twisted away. With one finger she gestured toward the floor of the den. "Smooth the rug," she mouthed.

Jessica walked into the den, dropped to her knees, and smoothed out the carpet. It wasn't like she'd *meant* to bunch it all up when she'd been vacuuming, but it had happened. Big deal. Why did her mother have to care about it so much? She decided she liked her mother better when there wasn't company coming.

"Oh, Ned," Mrs. Wakefield spoke softly into the receiver. Jessica could barely make out the words. "We've been through this before. I just think it needs to be a surprise for her."

Jessica froze. A surprise? A surprise for "her"? Who was "her"?

Mrs. Wakefield listened for a moment. "I know, sweetie, but you just can't talk about it," she said. "He said he'd be delighted to see her and—" She broke off.

Jessica held her breath and lay low on the rug, hoping her mother wouldn't notice her. She could feel her heart thumping like crazy. "He"? Who was "he"? And who was the "her" that "he'd" be delighted to see?

Mrs. Wakefield turned so that Jessica could just make out her profile. "It will mean the world to her, Ned," she argued, "but I don't think we can spring it on her now."

Dust floated around Jessica's eyes. She blinked furiously, trying to drive it away. Her throat felt suddenly dry. A faint hope rose within her, and Aaron Dallas's face appeared before her as if in a dream.

It couldn't be. *Could* it?

"She'd go crazy if we told her now," Mrs. Wakefield was saying. She laughed gently. "I've known her all her life, and I should have some idea. Anyway, they'll see each other tomorrow."

Tomorrow. A surge of excitement filled Jessica. It would be so cool to have Aaron next to her at the Thanksgiving table. If it *was* Aaron. But who else could they be talking about? It all fit. *Mom's known me all my life,* she thought, *and it would mean the world to me, and—* A speck of dust floated by her nose. Jessica could feel her throat tickling. She willed herself not to cough.

"That's what I told Aaron," Mrs. Wakefield muttered into the receiver. "I said he shouldn't expect—"

Aaron! Jessica wanted to leap for joy. But instead, she coughed.

Mrs. Wakefield swung around guiltily and started when she saw Jessica. "Well, I've said too much already," she said into the phone in a loud, brisk voice. "Little pitchers and big ears and all that. So I'll see you in a little while, then!" She hung up with a clatter. "You weren't listening, were you, darling?" she called out with what sounded to Jessica like fake cheerfulness.

There was only one answer to that question, Jessica knew. Standing up, she crossed her fingers behind her back. Inside, her heart was singing. Somehow, her parents had arranged it so that Aaron would be coming tomorrow, and they were keeping it a secret for a special surprise. What else could they have been talking about? She didn't know how they'd pulled it off, but it had to be true.

"Listening to your conversation? Oh, no, Mom!" she said innocently.

"No way are you bringing that into my room," Jessica said. She stood in her doorway, arms folded across her chest, and glared at the offensive object in her twin's hand.

"Huh?" Elizabeth wrinkled her nose. "It's just a CD, Jess." She showed Jessica the disc in her hand. "It's the sound track from the new Eileen

Thomas movie, *View from the Hotel*—"

"I know what it is," Jessica said frostily. Suddenly, she threw her hands up in the air. "Oh, for goodness sake, all right, all right." Elizabeth guessed that Jessica didn't want their mother to catch them arguing again and find some extra chores for them to do. "Bring it in, if you want to." Jessica flopped on her bed and started munching on a bag of pretzels.

Elizabeth put the CD down next to Jessica's stereo. Then she turned to her sister. "I'm worried about Kelly," she said.

"Why?" asked Jessica, her mouth full of pretzels.

"Jessica, please. You're getting pretzel crumbs everywhere." Elizabeth pointed to Jessica's bedspread.

"It's my bed, what do you care?" Jessica raised her eyebrows.

"You're right," Elizabeth said. "Never mind." *Never mind that I have to sleep in this bed tonight too,* she thought. *I'll just let it go. I don't want to fight with Jessica anymore.* "But about Kelly—I think she's not happy in Tucson."

Jessica furrowed her eyebrows. "What makes you think so?"

"Well, I was talking to Steven, and he seemed to think . . ." Elizabeth hesitated.

"Please don't tell me that you're going to listen to a word our *brother* tells you," Jessica said, with a look of disdain on her face. She leaned over to brush some of the pretzel crumbs from the bed to the floor. "If he knows what he's talking about this time, it'll be a first."

"You're probably right. But still, it must be hard for her, having a dad who lives so far away." Elizabeth pursed her lips. "It would be nice if she could find a friend here. Someone to make her less lonely."

"Well, we're her friends," Jessica said. "And Robin."

Elizabeth nodded. "That's true. We should make a special effort with Kelly—to be nice to her. And maybe Robin will too."

"Good idea! We can get Robin and Kelly to hang out together while we're off getting our hair cut today." Mrs. Wakefield had scheduled an appointment for the twins to get their hair trimmed later that day. She had said something about wanting Elizabeth and her sister to "look their best" for Thanksgiving dinner. "Maybe they could get to be really good friends. Like, best friends!" Jessica exclaimed.

"I don't know, Jess. I mean, I think Robin and Kelly will get along just fine, but I don't know if they're exactly—"

"Fine. Forget it. You don't like my idea." Jessica jumped off her bed and threw the pretzel bag into the wastebasket.

Elizabeth ran a hand through her hair. "That's not true, Jessica, it's just—"

"So you *do* like my idea?" Jessica looked hopeful.

Elizabeth didn't see any way out of this conversation without it turning into an argument. "Yes. You're right. Maybe Robin and Kelly could be close friends."

"Great. I think so too. I'm glad we see eye to eye, big sister." Jessica smiled at this reference to one of the twins' favorite jokes. Elizabeth was born four minutes earlier than Jessica, which made her, technically, the older sister. Of course, given their personalities, Elizabeth often felt like the older sister as well. "So, how will we do it?"

"Do what?" Elizabeth asked.

"Get them together. Get them to be friends."

"I—I don't know, Jess. You can't really make people be friends—"

"Of course you can. Don't be silly. We'll just get them to hang out together. They'll hit it off, I know it. I'll just tell Robin about all of the things that she and Kelly have in common."

Elizabeth looked confused. "What things?"

"Whatever." Jessica smiled. "There's bound to be something. Don't worry," she said as she crossed the room to pat her sister on the arm. "I'll take care of everything."

"Robin!"
Elizabeth dashed down the stairs and caught

her cousin in a big bear hug. "I missed you!" she said excitedly. She hadn't realized till this very minute how glad she was to see Robin again.

"And I missed you," Robin said with a grin. Her eyes sparkled, and her chin-length blond hair tickled Elizabeth's cheek. "As the adults always say: 'My, how you've grown!'"

Elizabeth laughed and released her cousin. She couldn't keep from grinning. Behind her, she could hear her mother running up. "Nancy!" she exclaimed, hugging her sister. "So good to see you! How was the trip?"

Elizabeth blinked. She'd always known that Aunt Nancy and her mother looked alike, but somehow they looked even more alike now than ever. Both had long dark blond hair and blue eyes, and their facial expressions seemed exactly the same. *Just like me and Jessica*, Elizabeth realized with surprise. The two women almost could have been twins, except that her mother was a few inches taller than Aunt Nancy.

"It's so good to see you too, Alice," Aunt Nancy said warmly. "It's been too long. And the trip was wonderful!"

"'Wonderful' isn't the word," Robin whispered in Elizabeth's ear. "Try 'long.' Try 'boring.' Try 'Stacey was incredibly obnoxious.'" She chuckled. "Anything but 'wonderful'!"

"How is everybody?" Aunt Nancy asked.

"Everybody is just fine," Mrs. Wakefield said. "Ned's gone to the airport to fetch Laura and Kelly, and they should be here any minute. Oh my! Stacey, is that *you?*"

"My, how you've grown," Robin and Elizabeth whispered together.

"My, how you've grown!" Mrs. Wakefield said in a hearty voice.

Smiling, Elizabeth turned to look at her youngest cousin. Stacey reminded her of Uncle Kirk, with curly red hair and freckles. It was funny how some kids looked like one parent and some looked like the other, she reflected. *Like in our own family*, she reminded herself. *Jess and I look a lot like Mom, and Steven looks more like Dad every single day. . . .*

"Yup," Stacey said. "I grew three whole inches this year."

Mrs. Wakefield swept across the floor and gave Stacey a quick hug. "Three whole inches in a year! My goodness!"

Robin turned to Elizabeth and said in a low voice, "Stacey thinks she's the world's next great playwright. She'll go on and on, telling us these stories she's writing that don't make any sense. Then she acts out all of the different parts. She's driving me crazy!"

"Hey!" Jessica appeared in the hall. "Robin! My all-time favorite cousin! How have you been?"

Robin smiled and gave Jessica a hug. "I'm doing great. How are you?"

"Terrific." Jessica flashed a grin. "And I'm ready to have some fun this weekend! I rented that movie you wanted to watch. *You* know." She wiggled her eyebrows up and down. "*Too Cool for High School*? Starring the ultimate in gorgeousness, Tom Drews!"

Uh-oh, thought Elizabeth. *I thought we already had this fight.* "Actually, Robin," she chimed in, "I was thinking more about, you know, a *thoughtful* movie." Elizabeth stepped forward, trying to get between her sister and her cousin. "*You* know. Maybe an Eileen Thomas movie?"

"Of course," Jessica said, glaring at Elizabeth, "lots of people fall *asleep* at Eileen Thomas movies. Before the first half is even over. But if you *like* that kind of thing . . ." She shrugged, and her words seemed to hang in the air.

Robin smiled. "I liked *Too Cool,*" she admitted, nodding to Jessica. "It was funny in a silly kind of a way. And Tom Drews is really cute!" She giggled. "But I really, really want to see *View from the Hotel Windermere.* All my friends say it's so well done, and the acting and everything . . . " Her voice trailed off.

"Great," Elizabeth said, relieved that Robin wanted to see the movie she'd chosen. "So we'll watch that one first. You can watch too, Jessica," she went on, turning to her sister. "And if we have time, we can watch *Too Cool for High School* later."

Jessica stepped back, her mouth a tight line. "Oh, that's OK," she said mysteriously. "I don't want to watch your movie." She smiled slowly, but it was a smile without much humor, Elizabeth thought. "I might just be too busy later this weekend."

"You might?" Elizabeth scratched her head. "Doing—what?"

"Oh, you'll find out soon enough," Jessica said. Fluttering her eyelashes at Elizabeth, she took another step back. "Let's just say that I think I'll have a lot to be thankful for tomorrow."

"Huh?" Elizabeth asked. But Jessica had turned on her heels and stalked away.

"Did I make her mad?" Robin wanted to know. She leaned against the wall, watching as Jessica marched upstairs.

"No," Elizabeth sighed. "I did. It's nothing but a little sisterly argument."

Robin nodded. "I know about those."

Four

◇

Kelly was trying to hide behind her mother in the front hall of the Wakefield home. She hadn't been back to Sweet Valley in a long time, and although she was excited to be there, she felt a little shy. Lucky for her, her mother was getting most of the attention. So far.

"Laura, you look wonderful," Mrs. Wakefield said, giving her younger sister a hug. "Doesn't she look wonderful, Ned?"

Kelly tried to look at her mother through the eyes of someone who hadn't seen her in a long time—and she realized that her mother *did* look good. She was pretty. So was Aunt Alice, for that matter; but dressed in jeans, Kelly's mother seemed much younger and more casual. Her hair hung down about to her shoulders, and her smile was a little crooked—*nicely* crooked. It occurred to Kelly that she never saw much of that smile while they were living in Sweet Valley, but her mom was definitely smiling now.

Mr. Wakefield placed Aunt Laura's heavy suitcase on the stairs and grinned. "She sure does," he agreed. "That Arizona sunshine must agree with you, Laura."

Aunt Laura smiled. "Sunshine? What sunshine? It's been gray and cloudy in Tucson all week!" she said with an easy laugh.

"Hey, Aunt Laura." Steven bounced down the steps and held out a hand. "Nice to see you."

Aunt Laura whirled. "Steven?" she said with amazement. "Wow! I barely recognize you! My, how you've grown!"

"Yeah, well," Steven said self-importantly. "I'm first string on the basketball team." Kelly wondered based on the shuffling of Steven's feet whether this might be an extension of the truth.

"Well, that's wonderful," Aunt Laura said. She shook Steven's hand vigorously. "Your parents must be very proud of you."

"Oh, we are," Mr. Wakefield said wryly. "Only we don't much like it when we get the grocery bill." He slapped Steven on the shoulder. "This may look to you like a normal American teenage boy, but it's actually an eating machine. Why, just yesterday at breakfast he ate—"

"Aw, cut it out, Dad," Steven said, clearly embarrassed.

Aunt Laura laughed. "I hope you'll leave some food for us tomorrow, Steven. I seem to remember that my sister Alice's mashed potatoes are truly a treat."

"You won't be disappointed," Mrs. Wakefield promised. "And, Kelly, how are you, my dear? It's so wonderful to see you. How are you enjoying Arizona?"

Kelly turned pink as Mrs. Wakefield crossed the hall to the doorway and wrapped her in an embrace.

There was silence.

"Answer the question, sweetie," Aunt Laura said.

"She must be the strong silent type," Mr. Wakefield joked.

Kelly looked down at her white tennis shoes. She felt a little overwhelmed. It was very strange to be back in Sweet Valley. *Everything is the same*, she thought. *Steven is taller, but he's the same Steven. Aunt Alice and Uncle Ned, this house, the streets we drove down . . . it's all the same. How can my life be so different when everyone else's hasn't changed at all?* Kelly blinked hard and raised her head. She tried, weakly, to smile

"Arizona is very pretty," she murmured. She made a real effort to sound cheerful. "I'm . . . glad to be here, though."

She hoped nobody noticed that there had been a catch in her voice just then.

"I'll call the girls," Mrs. Wakefield said, releasing Kelly. "You'd like to see them, wouldn't you?"

Kelly nodded eagerly. "Of course!" she exclaimed.

"And they're very eager to see *you*," Mrs. Wakefield promised. "Jessica!" she called. "Elizabeth! Robin! Kelly's here!" She turned to Laura. "Nancy is just getting settled in Elizabeth's room," she explained. "But I'm sure she'll be down in a moment."

"Coming!" Jessica called from upstairs. A door opened, and Kelly lifted her head to look at the landing. At the sight of Jessica, Kelly's face lit up. *And Jessica is exactly the same too*, she thought happily. She was glad to notice that she and Jessica still looked very much alike, although Jessica's hair was much longer than her own. *I'll bet Elizabeth's hair is longer than mine too, then*, she mused.

Jessica leaned over the banister on the upper landing. "Kelly!" she practically shouted, and hurried down the stairs.

Kelly laughed as Jessica pounced on top of her in a giant hug.

Mrs. Wakefield smiled. "Where are Elizabeth and Robin?"

"Off somewhere or other talking about dumb

Eileen Thomas movies," Jessica said, rolling her
eyes.

Another door slammed shut. Elizabeth and
Robin appeared on the landing, arms on each
other's shoulders. "Hi, Kelly," they said in unison, then looked at each other and burst out
laughing.

"Hi, you guys!" Kelly called up to them. She felt
warm inside all of a sudden. It was as though two
minutes in Sweet Valley had cured her of four mis-
erable years in Tucson. This was where she had
friends—and family.

Aunt Laura was beaming as the four girls tried
to give each other a group hug.

Mrs. Wakefield stepped forward. "Here, Kelly,
why don't you let me take your backpack? And
then all of you girls can go off and continue whatever it is that you were doing."

"Great!" Elizabeth said. "Come on up, Kelly."
There was a noise like thunder as the four twelve-
year-old girls thumped up the stairs.

Elizabeth smiled at her sister and her two
cousins. This was exactly how she'd hoped it
would be. They were all getting along famously,
catching up on old times. She was especially glad
to see that Kelly seemed happy.

"What would you like to do?" Elizabeth asked,
turning to Kelly.

"Well," Kelly answered. "I'd kind of like to hang out on that tree branch of yours for a few minutes, if that's OK." Kelly gave a shy smile. "I mean, if it's even still there? It was always such a quiet, peaceful place. . . ."

"Oh, yes! It's still there," Elizabeth said excitedly. "Do you guys want to come?" she asked, turning to Robin and Jessica.

"Actually," Jessica began, looking at Robin. "Robin said that she wanted to try my new Frostissimo Pink nail polish, if you guys don't mind." Robin nodded in agreement.

"I just love the color, and I can't get it in San Diego," she said, somewhat guiltily.

"That's OK," said Elizabeth. "We'll be back in a little while. Jessica, don't forget we have to get our hair cut in an hour."

"How could I?" Jessica asked sourly. "Right in the middle of our vacation day too. I swear—"

"Oh, boy!" Elizabeth smiled at Jessica's grumpiness. "Time to go!" She grabbed Kelly's hand, and the two of them went downstairs, laughing.

Kelly smiled and lifted her face toward the sun. It was so nice to be in this safe, quiet spot with Elizabeth.

"I sure see why you love coming out here to think, Elizabeth," Kelly said, turning to her cousin.

"Yes, it's a great place to be by myself—or with

someone else," Elizabeth said, smiling back at Kelly.

"It's beautiful. Like all of Sweet Valley. I've missed living here a lot." Suddenly, Kelly looked thoughtful.

"You have?" Elizabeth raised her eyebrows. "Don't you like living in Tucson?"

"Oh," Kelly said hesitantly, "I like it . . . most of the time. But I miss it here too. This is where I grew up, after all."

"That makes sense," Elizabeth agreed. "But it's good to have you here now."

Kelly's expression cleared suddenly. "So, Elizabeth, tell me everything that's been going on since I left Sweet Valley," she said, and settled back comfortably to talk to her cousin.

And as Elizabeth chattered on happily about her friends and activities and all of the tight spots Jessica had managed to get her into and out of, Kelly thought she could go on listening forever. *I wish I never had to leave*, Kelly thought. *I don't ever want to leave Sweet Valley again.*

"So, Robin," Jessica said, "do you ever miss France?" Robin and her family had only recently moved back to San Diego after living in France for a year.

"Sometimes," Robin replied. "Mostly I worry that I'll forget all of the French I learned. I wish I had someone to practice speaking French with."

"Oh, well." Suddenly, Jessica had an idea. "You know who's fluent in French? Kelly!" Jessica actually had no idea whether or not this was true, but she figured it *might* be. *Anyway,* she reasoned, *the idea is to make Robin want to hang out with Kelly. Once they do, they're sure to be best friends.*

"Really?" Robin looked excited. "Maybe we should hang out together and, you know, practice."

"Great idea," Jessica said, nodding.

"I wanted to talk to Elizabeth too," Robin went on, "since she's running that sixth-grade newspaper." Elizabeth and a couple of her friends ran a newspaper at Sweet Valley Middle School called the *Sixers.*

"What about?" asked Jessica as she dabbed a bit of Frostissimo Pink onto the last of Robin's fingernails.

"Well, a couple of friends of mine were interested in starting up a literary magazine. Mostly for poetry." Robin held out her hand and admired her fingernails. "I've gotten really interested in poetry lately. Thanks for doing my nails. They look great!"

Jessica smiled. "No problem. You know," she continued, "Elizabeth might be able to help you, but the person in our family who's really into poetry is Kelly!" *That is,* Jessica reasoned, *Kelly looks like someone who would like reading poetry.*

"Maybe you should talk to her about it. She's really into English—it's her favorite subject." *This last part*, Jessica thought, *is true.* At least, it was true when Kelly was in the first grade. Jessica didn't know whether or not it was still true, but she hoped so.

"I definitely will!" Robin said enthusiastically. "I had no idea that Kelly and I had so much in common."

Neither did I, thought Jessica.

Kelly and Elizabeth had come back up to Jessica's room, and the four cousins were having a fantastic time hanging out. They had been there about half an hour when there was a light knock on Jessica's door. Her father popped his head in. "Ready for your new hairdos, you two?" he asked the twins.

"We're ready," Elizabeth said.

Jessica, who was wearing only one shoe, started frantically looking for its mate. "I'm ready," she said, somewhat unconvincingly.

"So I see," Mr. Wakefield said, giving a sly wink to Robin and Kelly. "And how will the two of you amuse yourselves while the twins are getting their hair done?"

"Um, do you want to take a walk?" Robin asked Kelly.

"Sure," Kelly said. "It's a beautiful day."

"Don't go too far, OK, girls?" Mr. Wakefield instructed. "Let's get going, Elizabeth and Jessica."

The twins gave hasty farewells to their cousins and scampered toward the door. "This won't take long," Elizabeth promised as she paused at the door. "In fact, if you take a long enough walk, we might even beat you back here!"

"So," Robin began as she and Kelly strolled down the tree-lined streets of Sweet Valley. "I hear you're really into poetry."

"What?" Kelly asked, confused.

"I hear you're into poetry," Robin repeated. "I am too. I just love Robert Frost—don't you think that the way he uses meter and rhyme is amazing?"

"Um," said Kelly. "Yeah."

"Of course," Robin continued, "I've also started reading some more contemporary things without meter and rhyme, and I like a lot of that too. Have you ever heard of Rita Dove?"

Kelly wasn't sure what to say. She really liked Robin and wanted her cousin to like her too, but she didn't know what Robin was talking about. She was torn between playing along—pretending to know about poetry—and just telling Robin the truth. *But Robin seems so excited to talk about poetry*, Kelly thought. In the end, Kelly decided that she didn't know enough about the subject to fake it. *After all*, she reasoned, *she* may *dislike me because I don't like poetry, but she'll defi-nitely dislike me if she finds out I'm a liar.*

"Actually, Robin," Kelly said, clearing her throat, "no, I've never heard of Rita Dove. In fact, I don't know much about poetry at all. I'm sorry." She peeked out from underneath her bangs.

"Oh," Robin sounded surprised. "Don't be sorry. I—I must have misunderstood. . . . I thought you were a serious English student."

Kelly actually laughed at that remark. "No. You definitely misunderstood. I'm a seriously bad English student. I'm a serious math and science student, though. I used to like English a lot when I was younger, but not so much anymore."

"Well, *que sera, sera,*" Robin replied, smiling.

Kelly smiled back. "Exactly," she nodded. "Whatever that means."

"*Tu n'est pas serieuse,*" Robin protested. "Don't be shy. I know you're fluent in French."

Kelly turned bright pink. She felt like she was an utter disappointment to her cousin. But if she thought it would be hard to fake an interest in poetry, she knew it would be *impossible* to fake fluency in a foreign language.

"Not exactly. I speak a little Spanish. *El gato es un animal domestico,*" she demonstrated.

"What does that mean?" Robin asked.

"That means, 'The cat is a domestic animal,'"

Kelly said. "That's the kind of phrase my teacher is always making us memorize. But I somehow doubt that people in Spain go around saying things like that and, '*La cabeza es parte de me cuerpo*' all day long."

"What does that one mean?"

"It means, 'The head is part of my body.'"

Robin cracked up. "Very useful," she said.

"I hope not. If I have to explain *that* to someone, I *know* I'm hanging out with the wrong crowd," Kelly said, rolling her eyes.

Robin laughed again. "You're so funny!"

"I am?" Kelly asked. "I mean, thanks!" She blushed again. Nobody had ever told her that she was funny before. Maybe it was okay that she didn't speak French.

"Speaking of funny, who's your favorite comedian?" Robin asked.

Kelly thought about this for a moment. Now this was a topic she knew a lot about; Kelly loved comedy. "I like lots of comedians, but Lucy Billy is my favorite."

Robin looked excited. "Mine too! Did you see her last movie, *Mrs. Spitfire*?"

Kelly nodded her head vigorously. "Of course! I went the day it opened!"

"Me too. My friends and I had to wait in line for three hours to get in, but it was totally worth it." Robin started laughing softly. "That scene where she accidentally inhales the helium, and her voice is stuck sounding bizarre—"

"And she has to explain the secret code to the French guy?" Kelly broke in. "That was hilarious!"

At the thought of this, both cousins dissolved into laughter. Suddenly, Kelly stopped.

"What's wrong?" Robin asked. Kelly was staring at something. Robin turned to see what it was, but she didn't see anything except an ordinary house. Kelly knew that there was no way that Robin could realize that she was staring at *her* house, at the house Kelly had lived in when she lived in Sweet Valley. It had snuck up on her. She had been having such a great time with Robin that she didn't realize where she was going. But her feet had taken her down the familiar path to her old home.

"Hello? Kelly, are you with us?" Robin waved her hand in front of Kelly's face.

Kelly gave a sudden start. "Oh!" she said. "I was—uh—just trying to remember that other really funny part of the movie. Uh—where the French guy goes insane and thinks he's a poodle? Remember, he kept saying, 'I am a *leetle* dog!'"

"Oh, yeah." Robin started giggling. Kelly was relieved. She didn't want to ruin her fun time with Robin by dwelling on how much she missed Sweet Valley. "I—I think we've been walking for a while now," she said. "Let's get back to the house."

*   *   *

Kelly and Robin walked up the stairs to the Wakefield house. As they walked in the door, Stacey ran up to Robin. "Where've you been?" she demanded.

"I've been talking to Kelly," Robin said, and smiled at her cousin. Kelly smiled back.

"Can I hang out with you guys? I'm bored." Stacey rolled her eyes for emphasis.

"Well," Robin said, "we're not exactly doing anything right now, but sure. Why don't we go see what the twins are up to? Are they back from the beauty parlor?" she asked her little sister.

"They got back about ten minutes ago," Stacey said. Then she added in a whisper, "I think they're in a fight."

Robin rolled her eyes. "Oh, well. We'll go take their minds off of each other. Do you want to, Kelly?"

"Sounds great." Kelly nodded, and they headed upstairs to Jessica's room.

There were general bickering noises coming from behind Jessica's door. "Well, I *don't* want to listen to the sound track to dumb old Eileen Thomas's movie!" said a voice.

Kelly froze. She hated it when people fought. For a minute, she was tempted to suggest to Robin that they do something else. She looked over at Robin and Stacey. Robin looked back. "It sounds

like Jessica and Elizabeth have definitely found
something else to argue over." She smiled and
shook her head. "Sisters!" Robin gave one of
Stacey's red curls an affectionate tug.

"Oh, brother," said Stacey.

"Should we interrupt them?" Kelly asked, hesitantly. She didn't want the twins to start yelling
at *her*.

Another voice behind the door was saying, "I
should get to decide what we listen to because
you borrowed my lip gloss and never returned
it!"

"I think we'd better interrupt them," said Robin,
"before this argument gets so ridiculous that I die
laughing." She swung open the door. The twins
were standing by the stereo with angry expressions
on their faces. Elizabeth was holding the CD from
View from the Hotel Windermere in her hand. "Hi,
you guys!" Robin bounced into the room.
"Anybody mind if I turn on the radio?" Kelly hung
back, amazed that Robin could act so nonchalant.
But the minute she turned on the radio, the twins
seemed to forget they were in a fight. *I guess that
when you live with a sister*, Kelly thought, *you learn
how to deal with situations like this.*

"Hey, Robin. Hey, you guys," Jessica said with a
smile. "How was the walk?"

"Great!" Robin said, and Kelly smiled and nodded. "Kelly and I have a lot in common, although

not the things I thought we had in common." Robin raised her eyebrows at Jessica, meaningfully. Jessica began to cough.

Robin flopped on the bed. "So—should we just hang out here?"

"Let's," Elizabeth said. "I like just talking to you guys."

"Robin," Stacey addressed her sister, "if we're going to stay up here for a while, will you French braid my hair?"

"OK, but I'll need a brush and a ponytail holder or a scrunchie or something. Do you have any, Jessica?" Robin asked.

"Are you kidding?" Jessica replied, and stood up. She started rummaging around her room. By the time she was finished, she had laid four combs, three brushes, and a seemingly infinite number of barrettes, scrunchies, and ponytail holders of different varieties at Robin's feet.

"Wow! We could do everyone's hair in Sweet Valley with all of this stuff!" Robin laughed.

"Actually . . . ," began Elizabeth. "Would you do *my* hair, Jessica? I feel like getting it off my face after that haircut."

"No problem," Jessica said. "Sit here." She gestured in front of her.

Kelly watched as the two pairs of sisters did each other's hair. She felt a little uneasy, although she wasn't sure why. She stood up and walked across the room, pretending to be interested in something on one of Jessica's shelves. *I wish I had a magazine or something,* she thought.

Elizabeth's voice nearly made her jump. "Kelly, why don't I do your hair?"

Kelly put the seashell she had picked up back on the shelf. "Oh," she said. "Thanks, that would be great. Do you mind?" she asked, and looked at her shoes.

"Of course not!" said Elizabeth. "Just come and sit in front of me." Elizabeth grabbed a brush. "Pick out a scrunchie," she added.

"If you sit in between me and Elizabeth, you could do my hair while Elizabeth does yours and I do Stacey's," suggested Robin. "We'll have a French braid factory!"

Jessica giggled. "Hey! No fair! I'm the only one who doesn't get a braid."

"Well . . . we could sit in a circle," Stacey offered. "I know how to French braid."

"Great idea!" agreed Elizabeth. "Everybody stop braiding. Let's get settled and start over."

There was a general bustle as the five cousins situated themselves in a circle. Then they began braiding and talking and laughing. Every now and then, someone would laugh so hard that the person braiding her hair had to stop and start again. Then the person doing the braiding would pretend to grumble, which only made everyone laugh harder.

In the end, there were five heads with braids, some a bit more lopsided than others, and five cousins in very good moods. And Kelly, who had been sad for nearly four years and only hours before felt as though she didn't have a friend in the world, Kelly was in the best mood of all. Here, with these cousins she hardly knew, Kelly felt like she'd come home at last.

Five

◇

"Oh, I just love looking at these old photo albums," Aunt Nancy said to her sisters.

"Me too," exclaimed Aunt Laura. "Look at this photo of Mom and Dad—they look so formal!"

The three sisters sat around the kitchen table drinking coffee while Steven skulked around the corner in the dining room, listening to the conversation and adding to his family tree. Once they started looking at those old pictures, he knew that they would spill some juicy family secrets.

"And here's you as a baby, Nancy," Mrs. Wakefield said.

The next picture made them all chuckle to themselves. "Aunt Helen was always making those funny faces!" said Aunt Laura.

"She could make you laugh for hours as a baby, Laura," Aunt Nancy agreed. "Of course, you were her favorite."

"Oh, that's not true," Aunt Laura protested.

"You were everybody's favorite. Everybody's baby."

Mrs. Wakefield piped up. "You *were* the baby of the family, Laura. But I think that Aunt Helen liked all of us equally." They turned another page.

"Remember those plays we used to put on for Mom and Dad? There you are in your princess outfit, Nancy. You always got the best parts because you wrote the plays. Always in charge, from an early age." Mrs. Wakefield shook her head and smiled.

"Well, I was the oldest, so I felt responsible for you two. I felt like your second mother, sometimes," Aunt Nancy sighed.

"And we were lucky to have you to take care of us. Otherwise, we always would have gone off on Laura's crazy schemes!"

"Come on, Alice!" exclaimed Laura. "You two never would have had any fun if it weren't for me!"

The three sisters laughed. "That's true, Laura. Like the *fun* time you insisted that we help you dig a hole in our backyard so you could go to China?" Aunt Nancy teased her sister. "Dad was so angry about that huge trench we dug in the yard, we weren't allowed to play outside for a *week*."

"It really wasn't a very big hole," said Aunt Laura, and all three sisters laughed again.

"We did have a wonderful childhood, didn't we?" Mrs. Wakefield looked at her sisters.

"Yes, we did," agreed Aunt Nancy, as Aunt Laura nodded and smiled.

Steven frowned. He was worried that maybe his mother and her sisters really *did* have the perfect life when they were growing up. That wouldn't get him anywhere on his project!

Aunt Nancy looked around the sunny kitchen. "You certainly do have a lovely home, Alice. Honestly, your house should be in a magazine, it's so well kept! How do you manage to keep it so tidy with three active children running through it all of the time?"

"Well," said Mrs. Wakefield, "my children are active, but they *love* to pitch in with the housework. That makes having a clean house very easy."

Steven nearly gave himself away with a snorting noise.

"And when did the twins grow up?" continued Aunt Nancy. "I swear, they're such young ladies now. And Steven is the spitting image of your handsome husband!"

Steven grinned to himself, grateful that his Aunt Nancy could appreciate a good-looking guy such as himself when she saw one. *She has more taste than I thought.*

"You know," Aunt Nancy continued, "I'm so glad that our girls all get along. The twins and Robin have so much in common! Robin is doing wonderfully in school; she's getting all A's except for one B-plus in English, and that was only because of a misunderstanding between her and the teacher about the proper format for one of the essays."

"Congratulations!" said Mrs. Wakefield. "Then it's no wonder that she and Elizabeth get along so well. Elizabeth takes her work so seriously and is so organized—which is what makes her such a strong student. She's also the editor of the sixth-grade paper, the *Sixers*." Mrs. Wakefield smiled. "She's always so busy!"

Man, this is boring, thought Steven. *When is Mom going to talk about me? Who cares about Elizabeth's lame sixth-grade antics? Let's hear more about how handsome I am!*

Mrs. Wakefield continued. "And Jessica, she's a social whirl if I ever saw one. She's in a club called the Unicorns at school, and they're always organizing one event or another."

Steven rolled his eyes. Had his mother lost her mind? Jessica belonged to the Unicorn Club all right—it was an exclusive club made up of the most beautiful and popular girls at Sweet Valley Middle School. But the Unicorns weren't known for being sweet and friendly. In fact, even Elizabeth, who never liked to say anything negative about anyone, sometimes referred to them as the "Snob Squad." Jessica's dumb club was certainly not as important as any of *his* accomplishments.

"And did Steven tell you that he's a starting guard on the basketball team? They've won most of their games so far."

Well, we're two and one anyway, Steven thought. Like he always said, Steven Wakefield was worth bragging about. It was nice that his mother saw things his way for a change.

"Excellent!" chirped Aunt Nancy. "It's such a good idea to cultivate an interest in sports. My Stacey is a born athlete, like her father. One of the local diving coaches saw her fooling around in the pool one day, not doing anything fancy or formal, mind you, and he was so impressed by her grace and skill that he signed her up for his swimming and diving team on the spot!"

There was a pause. Then Mrs. Wakefield began again, "So, Laura, tell us something about Kelly."

"Oh—" Aunt Laura paused. "Well, Kelly's managing. Thanks for asking."

Aunt Nancy's voice echoed from the other room. "Well!" Coffee trickled into a mug. "I hope you don't mind my asking, but—is everything all right with Kelly? She seems sort of—well, a bit out of sorts."

She seems sort of sad, thought Steven.

"Thanksgiving's a tough time of year for her," Aunt Laura said slowly.

Steven suspected that every time of year was a hard one for Kelly, but he leaned closer so he could hear every word.

"That's right," Mrs. Wakefield said thoughtfully. "It was Thanksgiving time when Greg left you, wasn't it?"

"When Greg left *me*?" Laura repeated with a note of sadness in her voice. "You mean when I left *him*, Alice. Let's get that straight right now. Yes, I'd come to the end of my rope, and it was the best move I ever made. I only wish I'd left ten years before."

"Of course, Laura, that's what I meant." Mrs. Wakefield sounded apologetic.

Steven pricked up his ears. Here was some good juicy stuff. He opened his spiral notebook to a blank sheet. "AL says she left UG, not other way rnd," he wrote, hoping he'd remember that "AL" stood for "Aunt Laura" and not "American League."

"As I recall, Laura, I did warn you against that

marriage," Aunt Nancy remarked. A teaspoon vigorously rattled inside a cup.

"I know," Aunt Laura mumbled with a sigh. "Let's not go through all that again, all right, Nancy? I made a mistake, and I know it now. You're older, and I should have listened to you, and I—didn't. OK? You win. But I loved Greg. At least I thought I did. And there was that other situation . . ."

Steven scratched his back. It was only his opinion, but Aunt Laura had obviously been wrong not to listen to her big sister. As far as Steven was concerned, everyone should listen to their older siblings. To their older brothers anyway. "AN said no," he muttered, writing it down. "UG = bad news." Instead of a family history, maybe he should compile a tabloid paper. *News of the Wakefields*, perhaps. He could see the headline now: Why Greg and Laura Split Up— You Heard It Here First. With any luck, he'd find out next that his sisters were really descended from Bigfoot.

"Well, that whole situation was not handled well, in my opinion." *Aunt Nancy again*, Steven thought. "You always were too headstrong for your own good. Just because you got angry at Darren Caruso—"

"Darren Caruso broke my heart." Aunt Laura set her coffee cup down with a jolt. "I dated

Darren all through high school, and I loved him and I *thought* he loved me. But obviously, I thought wrong." There was a scraping sound, as if a chair was being pushed back. "We were planning on going to the same college! We were practically engaged . . . " There was a catch in her voice. "As you very well know. Until things fell apart."

"But that was no reason to marry Greg—" Aunt Nancy began.

"Maybe Darren had a reason," Mrs. Wakefield chimed in.

Steven held his breath and scrawled frantically across the page, trying to keep up. *Darren Caruso, huh?* Aunt Laura had been in love with some creepazoid named Caruso, and he'd jilted her, that much was clear.

"I remember it so vividly." Aunt Laura was obviously struggling to keep her composure. "It was April seventeenth, I even know the exact date, the date my acceptance letter to college came. I called Darren right away. His—his parents were away for the summer, but *he* was supposed to be home, and the phone rang and rang and rang."

She sounds as if she's going to cry, Steven thought.

Aunt Laura continued, "After two days of trying, I thought maybe something was wrong, and so I went over to his house, and—" She stopped abruptly.

"I remember that," Aunt Nancy clucked. "I *told* you at the time—"

"And he was gone," Mrs. Wakefield finished sympathetically. "But—"

"He was gone," Aunt Laura repeated in a thin, pinched voice. "And I never saw him again. Never. Not that I *wanted* to," she added quickly. "Someone told me he'd run off to join the army—"

"Marines," Mrs. Wakefield put in quickly.

"Whatever." Aunt Laura took a deep breath. "By the end of the summer, I was over him. I didn't even bother to ask his parents what had happened when they came back from their trip. I went off to college. I finally got a letter from him, about three months later, but I was so furious I—" She stopped again.

"Go on," Aunt Nancy prodded after a moment. "You what?"

"I tore it up without reading it," Aunt Laura said in a strangled voice. "And two more came, months afterward, and I tore them up too. He even called, if you can believe it, and I hung up on him. I didn't want to hear his excuses."

Steven leaned closer. This was great stuff. His mind raced. Forget the tabloid paper. His family stories belonged on *Phyllis Hartley* or one of those other daytime TV talk shows. All the same, it did sound like Aunt Laura had been treated kind of shabbily.

"But then you met Greg Bates—" Aunt Nancy said softly.

"I met Greg," Aunt Laura agreed. "He was the first man who took an interest in me after Darren. I was . . . flattered. He was handsome, and he seemed nice, and I was—well, I was all set to get married, I suppose!" She laughed bitterly. "I'd lost one bridegroom, and I wasn't going to lose another. Besides, I did love Greg. Even though I knew right from the start that he was completely unreliable, I thought he'd change. So I married him right away, and the rest is history."

"But you don't *know* why Darren didn't—" Mrs. Wakefield began.

"And I don't *care* either." Aunt Laura laughed again. "I'm through with men who aren't what they seem to be. And *that* is what I'm thankful for this Thanksgiving. That, and being back home with my sisters. With my sisters and their families." There was a pause. "So can we please just enjoy this weekend together?"

"You're right, Laura. I'm so glad you're here. And you too, Nancy," said Mrs. Wakefield. "Let's not spoil our visit dwelling on unpleasant memories." Aunt Nancy nodded her agreement.

Hear, hear, Steven thought. But he wasn't really listening anymore.

He was too busy scribbling down Aunt Laura's story.

*   *   *

"These pickles are dill-icious! I *relish* them!" Stacey cried.

Elizabeth laughed. She, Jessica, Robin, and Kelly had agreed to watch one of Stacey's one-woman shows. Actually, Jessica, Elizabeth, and Kelly had agreed to watch it, while Robin had grumbled something that none of the other girls could quite hear. But the other three eventually had their way, and they were now watching a performance of "The Girl Who Loved Pickles." It wasn't a bad show, and Stacey was a pretty good actress. By the end, even Robin grudgingly admitted that it had been good.

"Hey, you guys, where did Kelly go?" Elizabeth asked when they had stopped applauding.

"I don't know," Robin said. "She whispered to me that she had to go to the bathroom and slipped out. But that must have been half an hour ago."

"That's strange, because she really seemed to like the play," Elizabeth said, mostly for Stacey's benefit. Kelly had been smiling during the play, and Elizabeth didn't want her youngest cousin to think that Kelly had left because she didn't like the performance.

"Let's go see if our mothers caught her and are forcing her to tell them about school and stuff," Jessica said. "It'll be a rescue mission!"

The girls trooped downstairs in time to run into Mrs. Wakefield and her sisters, who were emerging from the kitchen.

"Hi," Elizabeth said. "Have you seen Kelly?"

"Kelly?" Aunt Laura wrinkled her brow. "Isn't she with you?" She leaned to the side and peered toward the stairs.

"Well, um . . ." Elizabeth licked her lips. "She sort of disappeared. We thought she might have come downstairs."

Aunt Laura blinked. She swung around to Mrs. Wakefield. "What's going on, Alice?" she asked, a note of worry in her voice. "You haven't seen my daughter, have you?"

Mrs. Wakefield shook her head. "What time was this, girls?"

"Um, like, maybe, half an hour ago?" Jessica guessed.

"Did she say she was going downstairs?" Aunt Nancy asked.

Aunt Laura blinked. "Oh, no. I never should have—"

"Well, not exactly." Elizabeth reddened and scuffed the toe of her sneaker against the rug. "We were watching Stacey's play, and she sort of left to go to the bathroom—and didn't come back."

"But where could she be?" Aunt Laura's eyes opened very wide. Mrs. Wakefield put a restraining hand on her sister's shoulder. "Do you mean that Kelly's *lost?*"

Suddenly, the front door opened, and Kelly walked in.

"Kelly! Sweetheart! Where have you been?" Aunt Laura nearly shouted as she ran to give Kelly a huge hug.

Kelly looked surprised that her mother was making such a fuss. "I—I'm sorry, Mom. I just went for a little walk around town. I was only gone a few minutes. I didn't think anybody would miss me." Elizabeth noticed that Kelly's eyes looked puffy—like she'd been crying.

"But of course we missed you, honey!" her mother protested.

"We all did," Elizabeth chimed in

Aunt Laura looked puzzled. "But where did you go?"

Kelly's eyes drifted to her sneakers. "Just for a walk. You know, around. Actually," she said, lifting her eyes, "I went to our old house. It's still there, Mom. I—I just wanted to have another look at it, that's all." She looked at the faces around the room. "I hope you weren't worried."

"You know," put in Aunt Nancy, "it's never a good idea to wander around all by yourself, Kelly. Not even in Sweet Valley."

"I'm sorry," Kelly said again, and her lip began to quiver.

"It's not a matter of sorry, it's a matter of safety," said Aunt Nancy. A tear rolled down Kelly's cheek.

"Nancy, can't you see she's upset?" pleaded Aunt Laura. "Please! Just let her get her bearings for a minute."

"Fine, Laura. If that's the kind of discipline you offer, then it doesn't surprise me that Kelly wandered off," Aunt Nancy huffed.

"I didn't mean for anyone to worry," Kelly said. Elizabeth noticed that she seemed very upset.

"Come on, Kelly," Elizabeth urged as she crossed the room to her cousin. "Let's go upstairs so you can wash your face, OK? And Jess, Robin, and I will fill you in on the funny parts of Stacey's play that you missed. "

"Yeah," agreed Jessica, "you missed some of the best lines!"

Kelly seemed comforted. "That's too bad. I'm sorry I missed it." She smiled weakly.

"Don't worry about it. We're glad you're back," Elizabeth said. She was relieved that she and her cousins were going upstairs. They definitely seemed to be escaping some tension among the sisters who "never, ever fought." Elizabeth just hoped that everyone would calm down in time for dinner.

Six

◇

"And then the gypsy princess finds a watermelon with a diamond ring in it, so she says to the elephant trainer—" said Stacey.

Steven sighed. He looked around the table at one of the most serious crowds he'd ever seen. So far, the only person who'd been talking at dinner was Stacey, but nobody seemed to be paying much attention to her. Steven guessed that this was because Stacey was describing the plot of her latest play in detail. It was kind of cute, but also kind of annoying at the same time. He glanced over at Robin, who seemed to be growing more and more irritated with her sister by the minute.

The side of Robin's face twitched. "Stacey, do you think you could skip to the end?"

"Robin," Aunt Nancy said with a warning tone. She had been silent for most of the meal, and the corners of her mouth were turned down in something of a frown.

"Mom, she drove me crazy all the way here with the misunderstood playwright routine; do I have to listen to it at dinner too?"

"Can I help it if Robin doesn't appreciate my genius?" Stacey asked.

"Knock it off, Stacey," Robin said, stabbing a crouton in her Caesar salad.

"Stacey, please. Maybe we can hear about the play some other time," begged Aunt Nancy.

"But I'm only on the second act of my twelve-act play!" Stacey whined.

"Nobody cares about your stupid play!" Robin yelled.

"Robin!" Aunt Nancy was shocked.

Steven was shocked too. *Wow, she's tougher than I thought,* Steven mused with a hint of admiration. *Not bad for a girl cousin.*

Stacey looked like she was about to cry. "Robin," Aunt Nancy repeated, forcing herself to remain calm. "Go upstairs. Right now."

"I'm sorry, Mom," Robin said quietly, and left the table.

"Well, that certainly was lively," joked Mr. Wakefield in an attempt to ease the tension.

"I'll go talk to her; she seems really upset,"

Jessica said in her best "concerned friend" voice.

Elizabeth nodded. "I'll go with you—I think she'll confide in me," she said.

"Oh, spare me! You think you're the only person anyone can trust with a secret!" Jessica was nearly shouting.

"Girls!" Mrs. Wakefield said. "What did I tell you about fighting this weekend?"

"But she started it," Jessica whined.

"Mom, Jessica is being totally impossible!" Elizabeth insisted.

Jessica's eyes grew wide. "Who asked you? Anyone can see—"

"Stop it right now." Their mother's voice was deadly serious. "Jessica, go to your room. Elizabeth, you go to Steven's room. Both of you stay there until I tell you to come down."

There was complete silence as the twins left the table, giving each other nasty looks.

"Wow, it's like Ten Little Indians," Kelly observed. "Who will be the next to disappear?"

Steven had a feeling that the next to go might be Kelly, but he kept his mouth shut. Clearly, his mother and aunts were not in the mood to be messed with.

"Kelly, that is not funny," Aunt Laura told her daughter.

Everyone at the table was silent.

"Here, Kelly, have some more food," said Mrs.

Wakefield. "You haven't eaten nearly enough."

Kelly just sat there, looking sad.

"She doesn't want any," Aunt Laura said tightly.

"Well, all right, sweetie," Mrs. Wakefield said to Kelly. "But, of course, I did make it especially for you." She looked around the table, a smile playing at her lips. "Remember that line?" she asked her sisters. "Any time Mom made something for dinner and somebody didn't take any, she'd look hurt and say—"

"'I made it especially for you,'" Aunt Nancy said heavily. "Yes, I remember, Alice. I think we all remember. . . ." Her voice drifted off.

The smile left Mrs. Wakefield's face.

"Why don't you tell us a funny story from your fabulous childhood?" Steven put in. *After all, I still have practically zero for my project.*

"Well . . ." Mrs. Wakefield strained to try to remember something. "Do you remember that day with the donkeys on our family trip to the Grand Canyon, Laura?" Mrs. Wakefield continued, with what Steven was sure was forced cheerfulness. "It must have been a hundred and twenty degrees in the shade, and sensible old Nancy sat in the hotel room—what were you, Nancy, about sixteen?—and absolutely refused to ride a donkey—"

"Well, it wasn't *exactly* like that," Aunt Nancy interrupted. Slowly, she began to roll a spoon between her fingers. She smiled brightly at Mrs. Wakefield. "In case you've forgotten, I was getting over a sprained ankle at the time, and I thought—"

"Oh, of course," Mrs. Wakefield said with a little laugh. "Whatever, as the kids would say. So, anyway—"

"It was not 'whatever,'" Aunt Nancy said calmly, but Steven could see her leaning forward across the table toward her sister. "It was a very real sprained ankle, and I didn't feel I should put any weight on it and—"

"You were injured," Mrs. Wakefield said with a nod. "Of course. Anyway, Nancy very *sensibly* stayed back at the hotel, but Laura, you and I decided to go, and we hadn't been on the donkeys for more than about ten minutes when you said—"

"It was at least half an hour," Aunt Laura broke in, shoving the rest of her meat loaf away. "Whenever you tell that story, the time gets shorter and shorter. You make me sound like some kind of a wimp, Alice, and I—"

"Half an hour, then," Mrs. Wakefield agreed, taking a deep breath.

She's doing a good job of trying to stay calm, Steven thought.

"Anyway, you said you were hot and could we go back, and the man in charge of the donkeys said—"

"I was too young for the donkeys anyway." Aunt Laura twisted her napkin in her hands. "I should never have been allowed to go on them to begin with."

Aunt Nancy laughed. "Why, Laura!" she protested. "You were begging to go. We didn't think it was a good idea, Mom and Dad and I, but you said—"

"Always headstrong." Mrs. Wakefield chuckled.

"Being headstrong has nothing to do with it," Aunt Laura protested, glaring at her sisters. "The point is, I was only about eight, and I wasn't responsible for—"

"You were always going off on some cocka-mamy adventure," Aunt Nancy said tartly. "Whether you were eight or whether you were eighteen."

Aunt Laura crumpled her napkin and flung it onto the table. "I *insist* that the two of you stop treating me like a child," she said, eyes blazing. "I've come all the way here with Kelly to visit you, and . . . and you're acting as if I'm still an eight-year-old—"

"*I'm* eight," Stacey chirped contentedly. "And I think being eight is just great!"

Mrs. Wakefield laughed uncertainly. "Now, Laura," she said, placing her hand on her sister's shoulder, "we don't treat you like a child."

"Certainly not," Aunt Nancy harrumphed.

"If you don't mind, I'll handle this," Mrs. Wakefield snapped, turning to Aunt Nancy. "Your style was never right for dealing with Laura—"

Steven took a deep breath. Aunt Laura was visibly annoyed by the words "dealing with."

This was positively painful.

Aunt Laura was being unreasonable, that was for sure. Who cared what had happened twenty-five years ago at the Grand Canyon?

Then again, Aunt Laura had a point. Aunt Nancy *was* so sensible, so—so sure of herself. What had she said? *"Mom and Dad and I,"* that was it. As if she were, like, the junior mom. And she was still acting like a know-it-all, telling Aunt Laura all the things she'd done wrong in her life. Steven could see how that could get old, *real* fast.

"Are you telling me how to talk to my own *sister?*" Aunt Nancy demanded.

"Of course not, don't be silly!" Mrs. Wakefield said with a little laugh. "Now, all I *meant* to say was—"

Steven glanced at his father, who was staring at his meat loaf, as if it might hold the answer to all of the fighting going on. The legs of Steven's chair bit into the wooden floor as he pushed away from the table. This fun little donkey story was taking a turn for the worse, and Steven didn't want to be there when his mother and aunts were asked to leave the table.

"Is everybody finished?" he asked before his mother could finish her explanation. "I'll clear the table."

Everyone stared at him.

"What?" he asked.

"I'll help you," said Kelly, reaching for an empty platter in front of her. Steven was actually starting to like her. *Maybe these girl cousins aren't so bad, after all.*

"See how easy it is to keep a clean house when the children pitch in?" asked Mrs. Wakefield brightly. "I remember how much fun it was when we did dishes together back when we were growing up. We'd laugh and sing—" Her eyes took on a faraway look.

"And tease me about my boyfriends," Aunt Laura snapped. "*You* may have enjoyed it, Alice, but I didn't. You two always stuck me with scrubbing the big heavy pots—"

"On the contrary," Aunt Nancy swept in, with a murderous glare. "As the oldest, most *responsible* sister, I had to do *far* more than my fair share of—"

Steven glanced at Kelly, who was rolling her eyes so far into her head that she probably had a nice view of her own skull. He smiled. "Let's get cracking, Kell. Our mothers are making this sound like it's going to be a mighty good time!"

"You said it." Kelly grinned.

"I'll help you load the dishwasher," said Mr. Wakefield.

"Ned?" Mrs. Wakefield asked.

"Now, honey, you just sit right here and relax. You made a wonderful dinner. I'll help the kids clean up," Mr. Wakefield promised.

I guess Dad can't take any more either, thought Steven. He glanced at Stacey, but she seemed perfectly content making sculptures with her mashed potatoes.

As Steven, Kelly, and Mr. Wakefield scampered to the kitchen, Steven could hear the Great Donkey Debate start up again. And he thought his kid sisters were a pain! Grown-up sisters were even worse. *If they never fought as children, they're sure making up for lost time now,* he thought.

Seven

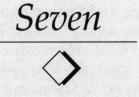

"So who gets which side of the bed?" Elizabeth asked. The twins were getting into their night-gowns in Jessica's room.

Jessica hated the whole idea of sharing her bed with her sister, but she knew they'd have to decide. "Let's see," she said. The left-hand side had the clock radio, but the right-hand side had a round table where Jessica liked to keep a cup of water in case she got thirsty. The coverlet bunched up to the right, but the left could be a little chilly now and then. . . . "I'm not sure," she admitted. "What do you think?"

Elizabeth eyed her suspiciously. "Well, if it's all the same to you," she said, "I'd prefer the right-hand side. I kind of like your table."

Jessica felt a flash of irritation, and suddenly

she knew she had to have that side. Elizabeth would put her books and tapes and stuff on the table and . . . and *contaminate* it, that's what she would do. "Well, as a matter of fact," she said slowly, "I think I need to take that side. It's better for my . . . um . . . for my allergies."

Elizabeth shot her a withering stare. "You don't have allergies."

"I do so!" Jessica's temper flared. "I get coughing spells all the time if there's smoke around me, and . . . and dust gets up my nose and makes me sneeze!"

"Which explains why you vacuum your room three times a day and keep everything so neat and clean," Elizabeth said. "You just don't want me to get first choice, that's all."

"Oh, that's not true," Jessica lied, coughing and rubbing her eyes to prove how allergic she really was.

A flicker of a smile played around Elizabeth's face. "Well, that's OK," she said, hopping into the left-hand side of the bed. "I figured you would want whatever *I* wanted, so I fibbed. I wanted this side, after all."

Jessica gulped. Her sister wasn't telling the truth, was she? No, she couldn't be. Elizabeth wasn't that sneaky. "You're—you're making that up," she said with more confidence than she felt.

Elizabeth opened the book she was reading and laughed. "You *wish*."

I will be mature, Jessica told herself. *I will be mature and grown-up and responsible. I will not throw my pillow at my sister, even though she deserves it.* She yanked hard on the coverlet and climbed into bed herself, coughing.

"Don't pull the blanket off me, please," Elizabeth said in a brittle voice. She snatched back the edge of the coverlet.

"It's *my* coverlet," Jessica snapped, pulling harder.

"Only because Mom is making me sleep here instead of in my own room." Elizabeth abruptly let go of the coverlet, and Jessica tumbled back against the headboard of the bed.

"Give me a *break*," Jessica muttered. She pulled the covers over her head and turned away from her sister. "Turn out the light now, because I'm ready to go to sleep."

"But I just started this—"

"Turn it off!" Jessica repeated loudly.

"But—" Elizabeth broke off. There was a pause. Then the light clicked off, and Jessica could feel her sister turning over and moving to the very edge of the bed. "Well, I guess you win," Elizabeth's voice sounded in the darkness.

Jessica smiled. *Ha.* She'd gotten to her twin. At last.

There was only one problem: She wasn't the least bit sleepy.

"So, um, Mom?" Steven asked seriously. His mother had just come upstairs after setting the table for tomorrow's dinner. Quickly, he stepped in front of her on the way to her bedroom and held out his notebook. "Is *now* a good time to ask you some questions about your childhood?"

Mrs. Wakefield paused. "Oh. The family tree," she said. "No, no, Steven, I'm afraid now isn't a good time." Her face brightened. "But later on this weekend—"

Steven couldn't help rolling his eyes. "Is now not a good time because it isn't a good time, or because you're fighting with your sisters?" he challenged her.

Mrs. Wakefield frowned. "Steven," she said, "you know that my sisters and I don't fight."

Steven spread his arms out wide. "Oh, really? What about tonight?" he demanded. "You were sniping at Aunt Laura, and Aunt Laura was sniping back at you, and Aunt Nancy was sniping at both of you—"

"Oh, Steven." Mrs. Wakefield managed a half smile. "That wasn't *fighting*. We were having a . . . a disagreement."

Steven snorted. "So from now on, I can just call

it a 'disagreement' when Jessica and I are going at it tooth and nail, huh?"

"Hardly!" Mrs. Wakefield gave a little laugh. "Children fight. Grown-ups have differences of opinion, as I said. You didn't hear us calling each other names, did you?"

No, I didn't, Steven thought. *But maybe it would have been better if you had.* He could just imagine his mother saying, "Nancy, you're a dork, and Laura, you're a dweeb and a half." Maybe they wouldn't have liked it, but at least their argument would have been over and they could have laughed about it and gone to bed happy instead of mad at each other. "If I were your parents, I'd have told you three to leave the table," he remarked. "Listen, Mom—just a couple of questions, OK?" He held out the notebook again.

Mrs. Wakefield sighed. "Steven—"

"Oh, come on, Mom!" Steven rifled through his notes. "Give me a break. First you spend, like, three days cleaning nonstop. Then you bring all those stupid *girls* to my house. Just one question, OK?" No way was she going to escape without giving him *some*thing. He glanced down at the notebook. The name Darren Caruso caught his eye. "Tell me more about this Darren guy who ran out on Aunt Laura, and I'll quit bugging you."

"What?" Mrs. Wakefield stood stock-still and stared at Steven. Her eyes flashed. "Steven Wakefield! What do you know about Darren Caruso?"

"Not—not much," Steven admitted, surprised at his mother's reaction. "That's why I'm asking. I only—"

"Since when have you been reading my mail?" his mother interrupted. "You know better than that! I'm shocked."

"What are you talking about?" Steven's mind raced. He never, ever read his mother's mail. Not since the time the sweepstakes people had sent her a letter saying she had just three days to claim a prize, and he'd called the number because there was a picture of a BMW on the front of the envelope. It turned out she'd won a bottle of shampoo worth a buck and a half or something dumb like that. And the long-distance phone call had cost, like, twenty dollars. No. Since then, he hadn't *touched* his mother's mail. "I didn't read your mail. Promise!"

Mrs. Wakefield pursed her lips as if she wasn't sure whether to believe him. "Then how did you know that name?"

Steven hesitated. "From you. And Aunt Laura. You said—" He consulted his notes. "You said she should have married him, and she said—"

"So you were eavesdropping instead." Mrs. Wakefield frowned.

"Well, not exactly." Steven swallowed hard. "I mean, you were talking in the next room, and I . . . I couldn't, you know, help overhearing." It was sort of true, as far as it went. Anyway, it wasn't as bad as opening somebody else's mail, which Steven was pretty sure was against the law. "You guys were kind of loud."

Mrs. Wakefield scratched the back of her neck. "Well, perhaps we were," she admitted. "I'm sorry, Steven. I just can't talk about Darren Caruso tonight."

"Aw, man!" Steven snapped his notebook shut. "What's the deal? First you won't talk about Greg Bates, now you won't talk about Darren What's-His-Name. What's the big secret, huh?"

Mrs. Wakefield smiled and put a finger to her lips. "Patience," she said mysteriously. "Good night, Steven." She hurried off down the hall and opened her bedroom door.

Great. Just great. Steven puffed his cheeks full of air and blew out hard. "Thanks a lot, Mom," he muttered.

So what was so mysterious about Aunt Laura's guys anyway? How come nobody would talk about it to him? For crying out loud, he was *fourteen* already. Practically a grown-up—with a girlfriend of his own and everything. If Aunt Laura had made a bunch of mistakes in her love life, you'd think the adults would want to tell him *now* so he wouldn't make them too. But noooo . . .

With a sigh, he sprawled on his bed, wondering what Darren Caruso had to do with his mother's mail anyway.

A little more . . . Elizabeth tugged a little harder on the coverlet, which she was liberating from her sister's grasp. She wished Jessica would go to sleep like she'd *said* she was going to. They'd been fighting over the blanket for what seemed like hours.

Jessica jerked suddenly to the side. The coverlet pulled off Elizabeth's left leg. An obviously fake snore issued from Jessica's open mouth.

Elizabeth sat up straight. She'd had enough. As Steven would say, "No more Mr. Nice Guy!" She tugged extrahard on the comforter and dragged it halfway off her side of the bed. To be safe, she gripped the edge of the cover firmly so Jessica couldn't pull it back. *Ha*, she thought, feeling mean and liking it.

Still snoring, Jessica wrapped her arms tightly around the blanket and yanked hard. In the darkness, Elizabeth thought she could see a glint in her sister's supposedly closed eyes. She tugged back.

"You let go of my blanket," Jessica hissed in Elizabeth's ear.

"You stay on your side of the bed," Elizabeth hissed back.

Jessica sat up, and in one lightning motion, she clobbered Elizabeth over the head with her pillow. "That's for stealing my coverlet."

"Oh yeah?" Elizabeth seized her own pillow and lashed out toward Jessica's head. But Jessica rolled away at the last moment, and Elizabeth only connected with her twin's shoulder.

"Ha ha," Jessica said. "Now you'd better be quiet, or Mom and Dad will come running in here." She grabbed the coverlet and lay back down with half of it over her body and the rest trailing on the floor.

If they go ballistic, it'll be your fault, Elizabeth thought. Hoping to catch her sister by surprise, she pulled the coverlet with all her might and turned to the edge of her side of the bed.

Jessica did the same. The coverlet pulled taut. Elizabeth strained her muscles—then suddenly, there was a snap. The coverlet soared out of her hands, and her body tumbled to the floor with a bang.

"Ow!" Jessica thumped to the floor herself.

Sitting up, Elizabeth winced with pain. She'd landed squarely on her hip. "See what you made me do?" she murmured angrily.

"Shhh!" Jessica commanded from the other side of the bed. "Mom's coming." Quickly, she clambered back into bed.

Footsteps sounded in the hallway. "If that's the girls fighting again," Mrs. Wakefield said meaningfully, "I'm going to murder them right now and save them the trouble."

"Quick!" Elizabeth lay down and adjusted the coverlet over her chest. "Pretend we're asleep." Jessica began to snore again. Elizabeth squeezed her eyes shut just as the door was flung open.

"They look like they're asleep," their father pointed out.

Someone switched on the light. Jessica snored louder. Elizabeth flopped onto her stomach, afraid the sudden brightness would give her away. "They do look asleep," Mrs. Wakefield agreed.

"Could that noise have been something else?" Mr. Wakefield asked. "A tree branch hitting the roof, say?"

"Maybe," Mrs. Wakefield agreed doubtfully. "It would certainly be nice if the girls would calm down and just . . . get along." There was a pause. "Is that too much to ask? This is such a stressful weekend, Ned. . . ." Her voice trailed off.

Mr. Wakefield took a deep breath. "Well, honey, maybe this wasn't the right weekend for the big invitation."

"But I wanted it to be a surprise, and this weekend seemed perfect," Mrs. Wakefield said with a sigh. "Oh, well. What's done is done. I guess we'll find out tomorrow."

The light vanished. The door clicked shut behind Mr. and Mrs. Wakefield.

Elizabeth stirred in the darkness, suddenly realizing how tired she was. It had been quite a day.

She yawned, wondering what invitation her father was talking about. . . .

Eight

Jessica opened her eyes and yawned. *Thanksgiving morning.* She stole a quick look at the clock. *Only seven-thirty. Way too early to be up.* Yawning again, she rolled over and buried her head deep in her pillow.

A voice floated up from downstairs. "Honestly, Nancy, I can't imagine what you were thinking!"

Sounds like Mom, Jessica thought sleepily. She groaned. First thing in the morning, and already it sounded like her mom was mad. Pressing the pillow around her ears, she tried to remember the dream she'd been having. *Me and Aaron were at . . . at Casey's, right, only it was, like, different, and he told me—*

"Oh, *Nancy* can take care of things."

Aunt Laura's voice, Jessica told herself.

"Nancy's *good* at minding other people's business."

Jessica rolled over again, dimly aware that three-quarters of the coverlet was at the foot of the bed. She grabbed it and pulled hard. Didn't her mom and aunts know how childish they were being? How could they expect her and Elizabeth to sleep through this racket?

Speaking of Elizabeth— Jessica frowned. Blindly, she reached out with her foot and probed Elizabeth's side of the bed. Nothing was there. *She must be up already*, Jessica told herself, yawning. What was the point of a holiday if you couldn't sleep late?

"But you *knew* I had a special recipe." Mrs. Wakefield sounded hurt. Somewhere, a door slammed shut. "I've made the same stuffing every Thanksgiving since Steven was born, and I don't—"

"I *thought* you'd be happy." Aunt Nancy's voice was strained and snappish.

Unable to go back to sleep, Jessica sat up and opened her eyes. The bedroom door stood wide open. Early-morning light poured into the room through the hall window.

"I *thought* you'd appreciate a little *help* around here."

"Alice doesn't need your help," Aunt Laura cut in. "You're so—so overbearing, Nancy."

"Overbearing!" Aunt Nancy exclaimed. "I am *not* overbearing. I just thought that Alice had enough to do with—" She broke off abruptly.

Huh? Despite herself, Jessica straggled out of bed and padded into the hallway in her bare feet. She couldn't believe her aunt had just said what . . . well, what she thought she'd said.

"Are you saying that my children are trouble?" Mrs. Wakefield asked coldly.

"Of course not." Aunt Nancy sounded tired. "You're twisting my words around all over again. And I wish you two would quit ganging up on me," she went on. "It's because I'm the oldest, isn't it? You've always resented . . ."

Biting her lip, Jessica arrived at the landing. Elizabeth sat there already, a worried expression on her face, clutching her nightgown tightly as she huddled on the steps. "What's going on?" Jessica hissed, plunking herself down on the step above her twin. She could see the three sisters standing in the kitchen, staring at one another angrily.

Elizabeth put her finger to her lips. "Aunt Nancy got up early and put the turkey into the oven," she whispered. "Shhh."

"Is that a crime?" Jessica nibbled a fingernail.

"Shhh," Elizabeth repeated. "She stuffed the turkey too. With her own stuffing from Uncle Kirk's family recipe, and Mom—"

"Mom lost it?" Jessica asked eagerly.

"Well . . . she didn't really lose it," Elizabeth corrected, shifting her weight so she could see better. "But I think her feelings were kind of hurt."

". . . and besides," Aunt Nancy was saying, "it's like the time when we were kids and you both . . . "

Jessica sighed. "This would be funny if it weren't our family."

Elizabeth shook her head. "It couldn't be funny," she said. "This is sad, Jessica. It's sad to see sisters arguing like this."

Jessica couldn't help a snort. "Says you, the champion sister-argumenter of all time." Was that even a word? If it wasn't, she'd just invented it. "Remember last night? And yesterday? And the day before?"

"You started most of those," Elizabeth pointed out. "And it's different when adults do it."

"Oh, it is not either," Jessica said dismissively.

Elizabeth turned to face her. "Is too."

What a stupid argument, Jessica thought, but she couldn't resist glaring at her twin and saying, "Is not." She folded her arms with a big gesture, accidentally on purpose knocking her elbow into Elizabeth's shoulder.

"Ow!" Elizabeth reached up to rub her shoulder. "Stop trying to hurt me!"

"I didn't try to hurt you," Jessica grumbled.

She didn't feel guilty or anything. Anyway, Elizabeth was faking, anybody could see that. "Your shoulder shouldn't have been there to begin with."

Elizabeth stood up quickly, her eyes flashing. As she turned, the hem of her nightgown billowed into Jessica's face. "*I* was here *first,*" she said, teeth clenched.

"Big fat hairy deal," Jessica said, slapping the hem away more roughly than she'd intended. "Get your smelly nightgown out of my face."

"Don't you push me around." Elizabeth teetered on the step before regaining her balance. "I'll push you right back."

"Who gives?" Jessica asked snottily. "I never touched *you.* Just your stinky—"

Elizabeth grabbed Jessica by the shoulder. "Cut it out!"

"I won't!" Jessica reached for her sister's knee. "One false move and I'm warning you—"

"Girls! Stop it this instant!"

Jessica froze. She looked down to the very bottom of the steps, where a large group of people was standing. Both aunts and her mother. Also Stacey and Robin, both bleary-eyed and yawning. *Oops.* Pasting a huge grin on her face, Jessica let Elizabeth's knee go, but not before squeezing it tightly. "We were just playing, Mom," she said brightly.

No one spoke. Mrs. Wakefield's expression grew more solemn. Jessica's jaw muscles ached from holding the smile. "Don't you believe me?" she said after what seemed like an eternity.

Behind her, footsteps thumped on the stairs. Jessica whirled around.

"Happy Thanksgiving," Mr. Wakefield said darkly, staring down at the assembled crowd. He stood above the landing looking unkempt in bathrobe and slippers. "Let's all *try* to get through the day without killing each other, shall we?"

"This is a totally dumb movie," Jessica complained. She waved her hand at the television screen. "I mean, look. Nothing's *happening*."

"Shhh!" Elizabeth turned and glared at her sister.

"Why should I shhh?" Jessica wanted to know. "It's not like anybody's *saying* anything." And it wasn't either, she thought as she rolled her eyes. *View from the Hotel Windermere* was about the silentest movie she'd seen. Every now and then, Eileen Thomas would press her hand to her chest, look worried, and murmur a few words to her leading man, but so far that had been about all the dialogue there was. Most of the movie had consisted of Eileen walking slowly through the woods, with lots of dewy spiderwebs and deer footprints and the Hotel Windermere looming in the background. "If I see another picture of nature at its finest, I'm going to barf," she grumbled.

"You have no taste." Elizabeth hunched closer to the TV set. On the screen, Eileen, in a fancy old-fashioned dress, hesitated for a moment in front of the hotel and then lifted the heavy old-fashioned knocker and let it fall. Old-fashioned raindrops pelted her old-fashioned hair. There was an old-fashioned *Bonggg!* and an old-fashioned butler slowly pulled the door open.

"Yes?" he asked in an English accent.

Eileen blinked several times. Rain poured down her hair and across her face. "A room, please," she said in a strained voice.

Preferably one with dewy spiderwebs and deer tracks, Jessica thought, groaning loudly. What a dumb movie. She wished she could go somewhere else, but she and her cousins had pretty well been told that they had to stay in the den while their mothers prepared the Thanksgiving dinner. *While they argue is more like it,* Jessica thought sourly. She could hear their voices faintly in the distance. Although she couldn't make out the individual words, she could tell by the tone that they weren't being friendly.

Uncle Kirk had arrived two hours ago, but Mr. Wakefield had taken him out in the backyard to discuss power drills or something. Clearly, they didn't want to be in on the fighting either.

She grimaced and looked around the room. Elizabeth and Robin were sitting close to the television set. It had been Robin's choice to watch this so-called piece of art. Jessica still chafed at the memory of her doofus sister grinning and wrapping her arms around their cousin when Robin had announced what she wanted to watch. Since Aaron was coming, though, maybe it didn't matter all that much.

In one corner of the room, Kelly huddled beneath a blanket, looking unhappy; and in the other corner, Stacey was scribbling away in a notebook. "Let's watch something else instead," Jessica suggested.

"No." Elizabeth's eyes didn't leave the screen.

"Oh, come on." A surge of irritation filled Jessica's chest. Her sister had no business telling her what to do. She gestured toward Stacey and Kelly. "I'm sure Kelly would rather watch something else," she persisted. "And this movie isn't appropriate for Stacey anyway." *So there.*

"Stacey isn't watching," Elizabeth pointed out. "Shhh. Here comes a good part."

Jessica stared at the screen. Eileen had paused in front of an old oil painting of a guy dressed like a banker or something, only an old-fashioned one of course. The camera focused in on her as she studied it, rain dripping off her nose onto the fine carpet of the hotel corridor. Then the picture zoomed in for a close-up of a single tear trickling down Eileen Thomas's cheek.

"That is *so* romantic," Elizabeth said with satisfaction. "See, the guy was her boyfriend, only he was too rich and important for her, so they couldn't get married. . . ."

Barf! Jessica took a deep breath. "Come on, guys," she pleaded. "Let's turn this stuff off and watch something *real*. I think cartoons are on now on channel twelve. Or we could watch *Too Cool*. . . . How about it, Robin?" Jessica put a friendly hand on her cousin's shoulder. "Let's watch *Too Cool* instead, what do you say?"

Robin wrinkled her nose. "Well—"

Elizabeth whirled around. On the screen, Eileen Thomas ran up the steps, sobbing faintly under her breath. Water still streamed from her hair and face. "Don't you guys like the movie?"

"I'm sorry." Robin leaned back against Jessica. "But I just don't like this as much as I thought I would. Let's watch *Too Cool for High School* instead."

"Smart girl." Before her cousin could change her mind, Jessica seized the remote and pressed the stop button. Eileen Thomas's wet face vanished in a split second, and a woman holding a can of lemon-scented cleanser appeared on the screen in her place.

"Oh, I just *love* this commercial!" Stacey leaned closer to the screen. "I think it's so well directed, and the acting is—"

"Be quiet, Stacey," Robin said, rolling her eyes.

Jessica yanked Elizabeth's movie out of the VCR, grabbed her rented copy of *Too Cool,* and fed it into the slot. "This movie is *so* great," she remarked, pressing the rewind button.

"I don't mean to hurt your feelings or anything," Robin said to Elizabeth. "Maybe we can finish watching it later, OK? It's just—well, it's kind of boring, is all."

Jessica rested her arm on Robin's shoulder. "Sorry, Elizabeth," she said, not quite able to keep the meanness out of her voice.

"Suit yourselves." Elizabeth stood up slowly. "Who cares about TV anyway? I think I'll go get a good book instead." She swallowed hard.

Good. Jessica grinned triumphantly at her sister. She heard the *whoosh* as the tape finished rewinding. Jessica clicked the play button, and the woman with the lemon cleanser disappeared.

"That was brilliant!" Stacey exclaimed.

"Here comes a *real* movie, guys," Jessica announced, wrapping an arm around Robin.

*   *   *

"Better choose what you want to drink with dinner," Mrs. Wakefield called through the door to the den. "Come on out, girls."

With a grimace, Elizabeth set down her book and stood up. She'd been sitting on the den couch pretending to read for the last hour while Jessica's completely stupid movie filled the TV screen. *What a dumb movie,* she told herself, *filled with dumb people doing dumb things.* There had been one scene where some guy was running away from a car. All he'd had to do was jump to the left or the right, Elizabeth could see that right away, but no, he just kept running faster and faster until the car finally bumped him onto the hood. . . .

Dumb.

Except that Robin seemed to be enjoying it. And Robin wasn't dumb. Not most of the time anyway. Elizabeth bit her lip as her sister and cousin stood up together, grinning. It made her feel . . . left out. Like she didn't count.

"Girls!" Mrs. Wakefield's voice was cross.

"Coming!" Elizabeth walked out to the dining room. The table was beautiful, she had to admit. Her mother had covered it with a deep blue cloth and set out a handmade centerpiece of pinecones, holly berries, and a single red candle. The table was perfectly balanced: one place setting on each end and five more on each side, all with a china plate surrounded by silverware. A napkin ring sparkled at the center of each plate. Platters of food lined the table, and there was a silver bowl of fresh cranberry sauce. In the kitchen she could see steam rising from a pot of potatoes simmering on the stove. Elizabeth's mouth began to water. At the same time, she half wished her mother had spent less time on the table and more time on relaxing. Maybe she'd be in a better mood that way.

"Yum." Robin inhaled deeply, smelling the delicious food. Jessica did too. "The table looks beautiful, Aunt Alice."

"Thank you, sweetie," Mrs. Wakefield said cheerfully. "I think we're going to get this show on the road, after all." She glanced over her shoulder toward the door.

Jessica smirked. She couldn't wait for Aaron to come walking through that door. *Any minute now . . .*

"Kirk, do you think you could get the carving knife and fork out of the top drawer, left-hand side?" her mother was saying. "We would be honored if you would carve the turkey for us today. Thanks so much. And, Laura, would you check to make sure everyone has enough—"

"Wait a minute." Aunt Nancy's eyes flicked around the table. "How many of us are there, Alice? Four of us and five of you—"

Mrs. Wakefield gave a nervous laugh. "Oh, don't worry about numbers, Nancy! We cooked more than enough for everyone. Now, please, check to be sure—"

"Oh, Alice," Aunt Nancy said wearily. "You've set twelve places, but we're only eleven."

Twelve place settings. Jessica tried to hide a grin as she stared at the table. Five on each side and two more, that was twelve, all right. "It's not a mistake," she said confidently.

Mrs. Wakefield glanced at the door again. "There *are* going to be twelve of us, Nancy. You see . . . I invited someone."

"Told you," Jessica said with a smirk. She elbowed her sister triumphantly in the ribs. "When's *Aaron* coming, Mom?"

"Aaron?" Mrs. Wakefield stared distractedly at Jessica. "You mean your friend Aaron from school? I thought you told me he was out of town."

"You mean, it's not Aaron?" Jessica's mouth opened and closed, and she blinked hard. "But—"

She stared at her mother's face.

Uh-oh. It was obvious that her mother wasn't kidding around.

No Aaron. The realization hit Jessica like a ton of bricks. Her hand flew to her mouth. She felt like crying.

How unfair. How completely, totally unfair.

*   *   *

"Don't keep us in suspense," Aunt Nancy said tartly. "Who is it, Alice?"

"Yes, who?" Elizabeth couldn't help echoing. Dimly, she remembered her father saying something about an invitation last night. But for whom?

Mrs. Wakefield smiled broadly. "I happened to run into someone on the street a few weeks ago," she said. "Someone I remembered from, oh, a long time ago. We got to talking, and, well, to make a long story short, I wrote to him and asked him to Thanksgiving dinner. And he accepted."

"But *who?*" Aunt Nancy demanded.

Mrs. Wakefield swallowed hard. "Darren Caruso," she said.

"Darren *Caruso?*" Aunt Laura whispered, turning pale.

"You didn't!" Aunt Nancy's jaw dropped as if a weight were attached to it.

Elizabeth stared. What were the sisters arguing about now? And who on earth was Darren Caruso?

"Wait, wait." Mrs. Wakefield twisted a once perfectly ironed dishcloth in her hands. "Listen, please, before you rush to judgment. I talked to him and—"

Aunt Laura tightened her mouth. "Why?" she asked. "Why did you do this to me?" She spun and headed for the steps. "No *way* am I eating Thanksgiving dinner with the man who broke my heart. Kelly!" she barked. "Pack your bags. Now!"

"B-B-But," Mrs. Wakefield stammered as she wrung her hands helplessly, "if you would just *listen*—"

"The time for listening is long past," Aunt Laura retorted. "He had his chance and—" She broke off. A tear trickled slowly down her face. Elizabeth frowned, reminded of the scene in *View from the Hotel Windermere* when Eileen Thomas had been staring at her ex-boyfriend's picture. "*Now*, Kelly," Aunt Laura said forcefully, and she stalked up the steps, Kelly following slowly behind.

There was a moment of silence. Then a door slammed upstairs.

"How could you *do* that?" Aunt Nancy turned furiously to Mrs. Wakefield. "Of all the tricks to pull—"

"I—I thought it was for the best." Mrs. Wakefield bit her lip. "And if she would only *listen* for a change. She's always so headstrong—"

"If you just wouldn't *push* her," Aunt Nancy chided. "Let her come to things slowly, that's the way to handle Laura. If you go springing things like this on her, then—"

"Well, who asked you?" Mrs. Wakefield shot

back. "I did what I thought was best. And if I'd told her in advance, then she wouldn't have come, and you know it!"

Elizabeth looked at her mother, then her aunt, and back again. She could hear Aunt Laura crying upstairs. Her heart thudded in her chest.

This Thanksgiving was turning into a total disaster.

Nine

◇

"I'm sorry, kids," Mr. Wakefield said helplessly, running a hand through his hair. He stood in the den with Uncle Kirk and all the cousins—except for Kelly, of course, who was still upstairs. "I'd hoped things wouldn't turn out this way."

Steven looked grim. What a great Thanksgiving *this* was turning out to be. Aunt Laura sobbing upstairs about this Darren guy. Aunt Nancy and his mother swapping insults in the dining room. His sisters fighting, Robin and Stacey fighting, and Kelly left on the outside looking in. He shook his head. *Women.* In the background he could hear his mother accusing Aunt Nancy of breaking some basketball hoop twenty-five years earlier.

"I still don't understand who Darren *is,* though," Robin said. She gripped Jessica's arm tightly. "Were they, like, going to get married or something?"

Steven listened as his father, with help from Uncle Kirk, told the story he'd heard yesterday afternoon: how Aunt Laura had been planning to go off to college with Darren and probably marry him later on, how he'd disappeared from sight, how she'd torn up his letters and refused his phone calls, and finally, how she'd married Greg Bates instead. "Darren Caruso messed up Aunt Laura's life," he muttered softly when the story was over. He still couldn't figure out why his mother had invited this jerk for Thanksgiving dinner.

There were a lot of other things he couldn't figure out either.

"Darren," Jessica groaned. "No wonder. It sounds so much like—" She clapped herself on the forehead. "I mean, if you say, 'That's what I told Darren,' it sounds just like, 'That's what I told Aaron.'"

"I beg your pardon?" Mr. Wakefield asked.

Jessica sighed. "False alarm. Never mind."

"But," Elizabeth said, frowning, "if Darren disappeared, how did Mom find him?"

And why, Steven wanted to add.

Mr. Wakefield sighed. "Your mother was out shopping a few weeks ago when a man came up to her. He'd heard someone call her Alice, and he asked if she was the Alice who had a sister named Laura. She said—"

"She should have said no," Robin piped up.

Mr. Wakefield shrugged. "Why should she lie? She didn't know who he was. He introduced himself as Darren Caruso. And when she started to push past him, he stopped her and asked—very politely—if he could buy her a cup of coffee so that they could talk. He was here visiting his family, and there were some things he wanted to tell her, he said."

"And Mom agreed?" Elizabeth asked.

"That's right. I'm afraid the story's—well, it's a little complicated." He took a deep breath and looked at Uncle Kirk.

"They're old enough," Uncle Kirk said.

Darn right we're old enough, Steven thought, annoyed. He settled back on the couch. "If there's a part that's, like, too mature, I can always cover my sisters' ears," he volunteered.

Mr. Wakefield rolled his eyes. "Thank you for your input. All right. Well, it turns out that Darren hadn't been admitted to college, after all. His grades and test scores weren't good enough."

Robin looked confused. "So he was stupid?"

"He was *not* stupid," Mr. Wakefield corrected her. "He was what's called learning disabled, only no one then had figured it out. He was a smart man who had trouble spelling, reading, taking tests, things like that, because of the wiring in his brain. His learning disabilities got in his way, and the college turned him down. He didn't know what to do. And, worst of all, he didn't know how to break the news to Laura."

"He should have just told her," Elizabeth said. "Aunt Laura would have understood, I know it."

"I agree with you," Mr. Wakefield said. "And Darren knows that now too, I guess. But back then, he wasn't so sure. So he didn't tell her face-to-face. He ran off and joined the armed forces instead. His idea was to work and get training, then enroll in college later on."

"He should have written her right away," Steven said, glowering. He took back what he'd said about Aunt Laura's life being featured on *The Phyllis Hartley Show*. No, it sounded more like a soap opera. "He shouldn't have waited three months—"

"He *did* write," Mr. Wakefield interrupted. "He wrote two days later, the day he arrived for basic training." He spread out his hands. "Darren told Mom that he mailed the letter and counted the days till she would reply. He'd written that he was doing all this for her, to please wait for him."

Elizabeth frowned. "But you said that she didn't get—" Her words hung in the air.

Mr. Wakefield nodded. "Yes. Darren's learning

disabilities came back to haunt him. He addressed the letter to Laura at 5820 South Appian Way, when the actual house number was 5280. He mixed up the digits. That's the kind of thing learning-disabled people often do without noticing."

Elizabeth sucked in her breath. "So the letter never arrived."

"And by the time it came back to him, marked 'Addressee Unknown,' he'd moved on," Mr. Wakefield elaborated. "When he finally got the letter, he realized what had happened, but it was too late. Three whole months had gone by."

Steven shook his head. What a terrible end to a romance. He sure hoped nothing like that ever happened to him. Darren was seeming like a nicer guy all the time.

"How awful," Jessica said suddenly. "Just because of two numbers getting mixed up. Aunt Laura could have married the love of her life, and instead she married the ultimate flake." She made a face.

Steven frowned. Judging from what Aunt Laura had said yesterday, he half suspected she had never fallen out of love with Darren. "So, why invite him here, then?" he asked, thinking he already knew the answer.

Mr. Wakefield gave an embarrassed half smile. "He's, um, single. Never been married. It sounded to your mother as if he'd never really gotten over Laura. He's had a fine career in the Marines; he's an officer now and a college grad—and he just happens to be stationed near Sweet Valley. Your mom said he was wonderfully charming and handsome too. She decided that . . ." His voice trailed off.

"That is *so* romantic," Elizabeth said.

Unbelievable, Steven thought. So his mother had decided to play matchmaker, not just peacemaker. That accounted for a lot of stuff: why his mom had been so compulsive, all the secrecy, everything. "She, um, wrote to him, right?" he asked stiffly.

Mr. Wakefield nodded. "She wrote to invite him, and he wrote back to accept. There may have been a couple more letters about details, I'm not sure." He looked at Steven curiously. "How did you know that? You haven't been reading your mother's mail, now have you?"

Why does everybody think that? Steven wondered.

"No, just eavesdropping," he said.

"Hurry *up*, Kelly," Aunt Laura snapped, thundering downstairs with a heavy suitcase in one hand and her purse held tightly against her shoulder. "I told the cabdriver to get here as quickly as possible."

"Laura!" Mrs. Wakefield stood at the bottom of

the steps. "Please stay—just another couple of minutes . . . "

Jessica watched from the doorway to the den, shaking her head. She'd never seen anything quite like this before—and she hoped she never would again. Elizabeth, Robin, and Stacey gathered around her, and Elizabeth rested her hand lightly on her twin's shoulder.

"You should never have done this, Alice." Aunt Nancy shook her head sadly.

Mrs. Wakefield whirled around. "No one asked you."

"We'll wait outside," Aunt Laura said, her face strained. "Come on, Kelly." Hurrying along, she stormed past her sisters toward the door. Kelly followed along with a duffel bag dangling from her arm—and an expression on her face that Jessica couldn't quite identify.

"Laura!" Mrs. Wakefield broke into a run. But as she caught up with her younger sister, a sudden sound pierced the house.

Dingdong!

"The doorbell," Mrs. Wakefield breathed. "That's Darren. Quick, Ned, let him in!" She seized Laura by the shoulders. "One moment, Laura, *please*. That's all I'm asking. One moment—"

Mr. Wakefield threw open the door. Mrs. Wakefield's face relaxed into a huge grin.

"Darren!" she said welcomingly. "Come in, come in!"

Into the front hall stepped one of the most handsome men Jessica had ever seen. Tall and dark, with closely cropped hair, he smiled tentatively around the room. "Hello, Alice," he said in a rich baritone. "I hope I'm not too late—"

"Oh, no," Mrs. Wakefield said automatically. "Not too late at—"

But Darren wasn't listening. Jessica's heart lurched. His eyes had come to rest on Aunt Laura's face. "Laura," he said gently, and smiled. He took a slow step forward. "Oh, Laura, I'd know you anywhere."

Jessica whispered, "Go, Darren!" She felt her twin's hand tighten on her shoulder.

Laura shut her eyes and took a deep breath. "Darren," she said in a tiny voice. "Go away, Darren. I've never forgiven you—" She clamped her mouth shut so tight that her neck muscles bulged. "Good-bye," she said brusquely, and turned away.

"Laura." A shadow seemed to pass over Darren's face. "It's been such a long time." He paused. "And I've come such a long way, just to see you. Won't you just talk to me for a minute?"

Aunt Laura was silent, staring at the floor.

Please say yes, thought Jessica. *Please, please, please!*

Finally, Aunt Laura looked up. "How could I

say no to you, Darren? I never could."

Darren's face flooded with relief. He crossed the foyer and wrapped Laura in the biggest embrace Elizabeth had ever seen. At first Aunt Laura seemed to sag against him, but after a moment she straightened up and her own arms encircled his body. And now, Jessica could see, both of them were crying, the tears flowing down Darren's cheeks and mixing with Aunt Laura's own.

Mr. Wakefield shook his head and wiped imaginary sweat off his forehead. "To the dining room," he mouthed, though Jessica suspected that Laura and Darren wouldn't have heard him if he'd fired off a cruise missile. "Let's leave these two alone for a few minutes."

A horn honked outside.

"The cab," Mrs. Wakefield groaned. She reached into her pocket and pulled out a crumpled five-dollar bill. "Give this to the driver, please, Steven, and tell him we've changed our minds, OK? And tell him Happy Thanksgiving," she added as Steven grabbed the bill and flung open the door.

Jessica breathed easier. It looked like Aunt Laura really wouldn't be needing the cab.

And it looked like it might just be a happy Thanksgiving, after all.

*   *   *

"I apologize, Alice," Aunt Nancy said a little stiffly as she stood in the kitchen. "*I* wouldn't have done it this way, but . . . well . . ." She gestured toward the front hall. "It seems to have worked."

"And I apologize too, Nancy," Mrs. Wakefield said, briskly spooning stuffing into a casserole dish. "I plan and I plot and sometimes I forget—" She laughed nervously. "Well, you know."

Elizabeth smiled to herself. *I guess now we know where Jessica gets that tendency.*

"I certainly do." Aunt Nancy smiled and bent low over the platter of green beans. "It's been one of your failings since you were little. Like my tendency to be . . . a tad overbearing."

"Exactly." Mrs. Wakefield smiled back.

"I'll take the potatoes out," Elizabeth said cheerfully. There was nothing like a bowl of freshly mashed potatoes still steaming from the stove. Her heart felt light. The kitchen was a mass of activity, the turkey was done, and Darren and Aunt Laura had been sitting quietly, talking, with their arms around each other, for about fifteen minutes. And, of course, Mrs. Wakefield and Aunt Nancy had begun smiling at each other again. "Robin, can you grab the gravy, please?"

"You know, Robin, you don't have to do it just because *Elizabeth* says so," Jessica remarked.

Elizabeth bit her lip. "I was just *asking* . . . ," she began. Now that the war between the elder sisters was over, it seemed only fair that she and Jessica should come to some kind of a truce about Robin. And about movies. And sleeping in the same bed. And . . . and everything. Grimly, she walked into the dining room. Why did Jessica have to be so difficult all the time?

"Who put out name cards?" Mr. Wakefield asked. He was already at the table, preparing to get everyone settled in.

"I did," Jessica called brightly from the kitchen. "Just now. It's to make sure that Aunt Laura and, um, a certain person get to sit by each other."

"Have some brussels sprouts," Mrs. Wakefield said, passing the plate to Jessica.

Jessica shuddered. "No, thanks." Aunt Laura gave Jessica a sympathetic look from across the table, then turned to smile at Darren as he patted her hand. The family had all just sat down to dinner.

Jessica took a quick look around and noticed something immediately. She frowned.

"Hey, Mom?" Jessica turned to her mother. "Where's Kelly?"

"Kelly?" Her mother pulled herself away from a conversation with Aunt Nancy. Uncle Kirk paused in his turkey carving at one head of the table. "Is she upstairs?" he asked.

Jessica shook her head. "I don't think so."

"Uh-oh." There was a frown on Mrs. Wakefield's face. She raised her voice slightly. "Has anybody seen Kelly?"

For a moment, no one spoke. Then Aunt Laura looked across the table at Mrs. Wakefield. "Oh, no," she said.

"It's OK," volunteered Elizabeth, pushing back from the table. "I think I know where she is."

Ten

◇

"Kelly?"

Jessica leaned down and touched her cousin on the shoulder. Kelly sat on the curb, staring vacantly at her old house, silent tears trickling down her face. "Kelly?" Jessica repeated when there was no response.

"Go away." Kelly leaned forward and buried her head in her arms.

Jessica took a deep breath. "Kelly, it's me, Jessica. And Elizabeth and Robin," she added quickly. "We've come because—because we want to talk to you."

"Please, just leave me alone." Kelly hunched further forward, shaking Jessica's arm off her shoulder.

Jessica looked to the others for help.

"Kelly, please tell us what's wrong." Elizabeth squatted in the street near Kelly's feet.

"We really want to help," Robin added.

Elizabeth sat down by Kelly. "We care about you," she said.

Kelly took a deep breath. "I know. I'm sorry. Sometimes I forget what it's like to have friends." She smiled up at them through her tears and tried to wipe them off her streaky face.

"What do you mean?" asked Elizabeth. Gently, she stroked Kelly's back.

Kelly's eyes filled with tears again. "I just miss Sweet Valley so much. I'm really lonely in Tucson. I haven't made any friends there."

"You must have friends . . . ," Jessica started, then bit her lip. "I mean, we're your friends."

"Yes, and you're *here*." Kelly's mouth twisted. "Not in Tucson. You have to understand—everything good that ever happened to me happened right here in Sweet Valley. I had friends here. I had a dad here. I have nothing in Arizona but my mom."

Elizabeth tried to comfort her. "But you're our cousin. We're all family together—"

"Don't you get it?" Kelly sat straight up. Angrily, she stared at her cousins. "I don't *have* a family. *You* aren't my family. I see you, what, once every couple of years? All I have is my mom. . . . " Fresh tears slid down her face. "And sometimes she's more like a friend than a mother. And now there's—"

"Now there's what?" Jessica asked gently.

"Can't you guess?" Kelly's eyes flashed. "It's—it's *him*."

"Him?" Robin frowned. "Who?"

"Darren, of course!" Furiously, Kelly stood up and shook off her cousins. "I told you I had only one friend in Tucson," she snapped. "My mom. Now she's going gaga for Darren. You wait. She'll get so fixated on him, she'll—" She broke off.

"She'll what?" Jessica asked curiously, staring up at Kelly from her position on the curb.

Kelly's lip trembled. "She'll stop having time for me," she said in a pitifully small voice.

"That won't happen," Elizabeth assured her after a moment's pause. "I'm sure it won't."

"Elizabeth's right," Jessica added awkwardly, feeling truly sympathetic for Kelly for perhaps the first time since she'd arrived. "It's not like your mom will just disappear. I mean, she's your mom." Even as she spoke, though, she remembered that Kelly's dad sort of *had* disappeared from her life. Another wave of sympathy washed over Jessica.

A small voice piped up behind them. "Can I tell you my latest story?"

The four cousins looked up. Standing behind all of them was Stacey, her curly red hair gleaming in the sun. "It might make you feel better."

Robin sounded tired. "Stacey, we're having an important conversation right now. Please go back home."

Stacey hung her head. She turned to go, her sad little shoulders slumped.

"No—wait," Kelly said softly. "Wait, Stacey. I want to hear your story. It's OK," she said to the others.

"Are you kidding?" Robin whispered as Stacey skipped over excitedly. "Once she gets started, she'll never stop."

"At least it'll take my mind off of things for a few minutes," Kelly said, "before I have to go back."

"This story is called 'The Rag Doll,'" Stacey began. "I already have some ideas for costumes and stage directions for when I make this into a play," she added to the four older girls. "Ahem. 'The Rag Doll.' By me. Once upon a time, there was a lonely girl who lived in a tower all by herself. She didn't have any brothers or sisters. She had nobody to play with. All she had was a bunch of rags. One day, she took some of the rags and made them into a doll. She drew a smiling face on the doll and named it Zelda. The girl played with the doll for a long time, and she forgot that she was lonely." Stacey paused and looked around. Everyone, even Robin, was paying attention.

"One day, the girl noticed that a beautiful silver

butterfly was caught in a spiderweb in the corner of her tower. The girl felt sorry for it, so she set it free. The butterfly flew around the room, then landed on the windowsill. 'Because you have set me free,' it said to the girl, 'I will give you your heart's desire.' Then it flew away.

"'How strange,' the girl said to herself, 'I've never seen a talking butterfly before.'

"'Me either,' said a voice from across the room. It was the rag doll! She was a real girl! And the two girls lived happily ever after, like sisters, and neither one was lonely ever again."

Stacey finished and there was a pause.

"That was a great story, Stacey," Kelly said. She smiled at the others. "Now I think I'm ready to go back."

"Well, this is turning out nicely, Alice," Aunt Nancy snapped.

"Well, of course you have the answers to everything!" Mrs. Wakefield retorted.

"Neither one of you understands!" Aunt Laura said helplessly. "Kelly is just like I was when I was younger—"

Steven stood listening to his mother and his aunts fight. They just didn't get it, did they? He glanced at his watch, hoping that the girls would return right away with Kelly. They'd had enough time to get over to Hudson Terrace and back, with some talking in between.

"Don't blame *my* girls," Aunt Nancy said, shoving her chair angrily away from the table. "*We* don't live here. *We* can't be Kelly's hosts all the time."

"No one is *asking* your daughters to be Kelly's hosts," Mrs. Wakefield argued. "All I'm trying to say is . . ."

The three men had retired to the living room, Steven noticed. He was wondering if he should do the same. And where was Stacey? Probably upstairs, working on her latest masterpiece.

"And why is it that Kelly is running off all of the time?" Aunt Nancy turned to Aunt Laura with a glare. "I wonder where she picked up that behavior!"

"Nancy, that is not nice," Mrs. Wakefield warned.

"Terrific—take her side!" Aunt Nancy replied. "Just like when Laura broke my collector's edition Harry the Hamster cup!"

"That happened when you were eleven years old!" Mrs. Wakefield banged her hand down on the table. "And it's not like Laura did it on purpose!"

"That is not the point!" Aunt Nancy shouted. "The point is that it was my favorite glass, and I could never, ever replace it, and she broke it!"

"We have been having this argument for decades!" Now Aunt Laura turned on Aunt Nancy, eyes blazing. "I'm sorry I broke your stupid cup! It was an accident. Do we have to discuss it now? Can't you see that I'm upset?"

Hurry up, girls, Steven thought impatiently, glaring at his watch. He suspected there'd be blood on the floor if Kelly didn't show up soon.

"Your problem is, you see everything as if it's only a matter of feelings," Aunt Nancy said. "Now, if you'd be reasonable for a change—"

"Look who's talking!" Mrs. Wakefield interrupted.

"What *neither* of you understands is . . . ," Aunt Laura began.

There was the sound of voices on the porch. *At last!* Steven breathed a sigh of relief. "Cut it out!" he bellowed in his loudest voice. "Truce! Time out! End of argument!" He stole a quick look over his shoulder. Yes, it was the three girls—and Kelly. "Look who's back."

If this weekend didn't get him an A for his family stories, nothing would!

"Kelly!" Aunt Laura rushed to her side and caught her up in her arms. "Where were you? I've been so worried! Please don't do that ever, ever again."

"Hi, Mom." Kelly hugged back but released her mother quickly. "You've been arguing again, haven't you?" she demanded.

Aunt Laura looked at her sisters. "Just a little . . . disagreement," she said slowly.

Elizabeth couldn't help rolling her eyes.

"Listen." Kelly swallowed hard. "I was out . . . thinking. Just thinking. And feeling sad. Which I still am," she added quickly. "Then these guys came and found me," she went on, "and this one"—she mussed Stacey's hair—"told me an incredible story, which proved something very important to me."

"Really?" Aunt Nancy glanced up at Elizabeth. "What was it?"

Kelly cleared her throat and pushed her hair back out of her eyes. "Look, I'd love to have a sister. Having a sister means having someone who knows you well. Who loves you." She dropped her eyes toward the floor. "On the walk home, these guys agreed that they don't know how lucky they are to have sisters. They don't appreciate having sisters. They've been arguing since we got here, and . . . " Her voice trailed off.

Elizabeth nodded. Stacey's story had make it clear to all of them how important it was to have friends—and how valuable a sister is. What had she and Jessica been arguing about anyway? It all seemed so unimportant now. Having a sister was like having a built-in friend, she realized. Well, she'd always known it, but it had taken Kelly, and Stacey, to point it out to her.

"You don't have to like your sister all the

time," Kelly said huskily. "But—but having a sister is one of the most special things anybody can have. And for the past few days, I've been jealous. Jealous and sad. Jealous of my cousins who *do* have sisters." She paused. "Because they're not . . . alone."

"You are not alone, Kelly," Aunt Laura said with determination, squeezing her daughter's hand.

"It's different with moms," Jessica murmured. She smiled faintly at Elizabeth, and Elizabeth found herself smiling back.

"It *is* different," Aunt Nancy agreed unexpectedly. "Sometimes I felt more like your mother than like your sister, Laura. . . ." Her voice trailed off. "And yours, Alice. And I don't fight that feeling very well, I guess."

"But I also felt mad," Kelly went on, her voice growing more confident. "Mad because you guys didn't know what you had. None of you! Mad because you kept trying to throw it away with all your arguing and stuff." She took a deep breath. "You complain about each other, and you fight, and you argue about what things were like when you were growing up. . . . But if you had to spend even *one day* without a sister, you'd be sorry. And you'd never complain again." She hugged her mother. "And . . . and I guess that's all I have to say," she finished, beginning to sob.

"Oh, Kelly," Aunt Laura said.

"I—I understand what you're saying, Kelly," Mrs. Wakefield said haltingly. "I hadn't thought about it that way before." She laughed uncertainly. "I do behave a little as if we were still kids, don't I? Pretending that everything's just fine, even when it isn't. Even when that hurts other people's feelings." She looked at Aunt Nancy. "And I guess that's something *I* need to work on. Because you and Laura are—" She swallowed hard. "Two of the most important people in my life," she finished in a choked voice.

There was silence. Elizabeth blinked back tears, for no reason that she could think of.

"And I—I guess I fly off the handle too much," Aunt Laura said softly, stroking her daughter's back. "I jump to conclusions, and I have too much pride." She held Kelly tight. "Headstrong, as someone said. But you're right, Kelly. I'm lucky to have sisters, even when they aggravate me and I aggravate them. I can't imagine not having them."

"Alice." Aunt Nancy stood up suddenly and stretched out her arms. Without saying another word, she and Mrs. Wakefield walked together toward Aunt Laura, and she joined the hug. Elizabeth could see tears in her mother's eyes.

"You know," Jessica began, "having first cousins is a little like having sisters." She grabbed Robin and Elizabeth and thrust them toward Kelly. "The three of us, I mean, the four of us"—she pulled Stacey next to her—"we're like your sisters too. Your extended sisters, Kelly."

"Hey, yeah." Elizabeth grinned and took Kelly by the hand, guiding her gently away from the three adults. "If you think about it that way, Kelly, you've got four sisters. And a brother," she added, remembering Steven.

"Really," Robin agreed.

"Five sisters," Steven grumbled. "Great. Just what I wanted." But Elizabeth could see that even he was grinning a little.

Kelly reached out to grab Robin, Jessica, and Elizabeth by the shoulders. "Thanks, guys," she whispered. "Thanks."

Elizabeth held on tight. "Thank *you*," she whispered. And she meant it. If it hadn't been for Kelly, she never would have made peace with Jessica.

Of course, it still wasn't going to be easy to share a room with her sister over the next few days. But at least now they had a chance of making it without killing each other, right?

"And, hey," Elizabeth whispered to Kelly, "don't forget that a certain *someone*"—she indicated Darren Caruso with a nod of her head—"lives near Sweet Valley. And if a certain *mother* likes him enough, she might just have to move back."

"Good point!" Kelly grinned. "I hadn't thought of that!"

"A toast," Uncle Kirk proposed, lifting his glass high. "To family!"

"To family!" everyone repeated. Jessica took a sip of juice and beamed at her cousins. Thanksgiving dinner had started up again, and even though the food was kind of cold, she didn't even mind. It seemed . . . somehow *important* to all be sitting together again. She turned to Kelly, who was now sitting next to her. Elizabeth could have Robin. At least temporarily. "I'm glad you're back," she said sincerely. "So, who's your favorite rock singer anyway?"

Kelly smiled shyly. "Johnny Buck?"

Cool. "To Johnny Buck!" Jessica cried, raising her glass.

"To Johnny Buck!" everyone chimed in, although Jessica noticed that her father was rolling his eyes. She giggled.

Darren slipped his arm through Aunt Laura's. "To Laura," he said shyly. "And to her wonderful family, who made this possible."

Jessica sighed contentedly. It was too bad that it hadn't been Aaron who was coming to dinner. *But let's be honest,* she told herself sharply. *You'll see Aaron again in just a few days. And what's a few days compared to all the years Darren and Aunt Laura were apart?*

A drop in the bucket, that's what.

In fact, Darren seemed like a truly nice guy. Strange as it seemed, she wasn't sorry that it was Darren, not Aaron, who had come over. And who knew what might happen next between Darren and Laura—now that the ice was broken again?

"Can we finish eating now, please?" Steven asked.

"Not yet." Mrs. Wakefield looked to her sisters. "There's one more toast that we need to propose."

"Yes, let's," Aunt Nancy agreed. Aunt Laura said nothing, but her eyes sparkled. Together the three women lifted their glasses high above the blue cloth of the Thanksgiving table.

"To sisters!" they said with one voice.

And to sisterhood, Jessica thought happily, clinking glasses with Kelly.

Jessica is stuck in Christmas Eve! Will she find a way to make Christmas arrive, or will she have to live the same day over and over—forever? Find out in Sweet Valley Twins Super #11, **The Year without Christmas.**

Jessica and Elizabeth are getting along now, but they're about to have their biggest fight ever! Find out why in Sweet Valley Twins #112, **If Looks Could Kill.**

Bantam Books in the SWEET VALLEY TWINS series.
Ask your bookseller for the books you have missed.

#1	BEST FRIENDS	#24	JUMPING TO CONCLUSIONS
#2	TEACHER'S PET	#25	STANDING OUT
#3	THE HAUNTED HOUSE	#26	TAKING CHARGE·
#4	CHOOSING SIDES	#27	TEAMWORK
#5	SNEAKING OUT	#28	APRIL FOOL!
#6	THE NEW GIRL	#29	JESSICA AND THE BRAT ATTACK
#7	THREE'S A CROWD	#30	PRINCESS ELIZABETH
#8	FIRST PLACE	#31	JESSICA'S BAD IDEA
#9	AGAINST THE RULES	#32	JESSICA ONSTAGE
#10	ONE OF THE GANG	#33	ELIZABETH'S NEW HERO
#11	BURIED TREASURE	#34	JESSICA, THE ROCK STAR
#12	KEEPING SECRETS	#35	AMY'S PEN PAL
#13	STRETCHING THE TRUTH	#36	MARY IS MISSING
#14	TUG OF WAR	#37	THE WAR BETWEEN THE TWINS
#15	THE OLDER BOY	#38	LOIS STRIKES BACK
#16	SECOND BEST	#39	JESSICA AND THE MONEY MIX-UP
#17	BOYS AGAINST GIRLS	#40	DANNY MEANS TROUBLE
#18	CENTER OF ATTENTION	#41	THE TWINS GET CAUGHT
#19	THE BULLY	#42	JESSICA'S SECRET
#20	PLAYING HOOKY	#43	ELIZABETH'S FIRST KISS
#21	LEFT BEHIND	#44	AMY MOVES IN
#22	OUT OF PLACE	#45	LUCY TAKES THE REINS
#23	CLAIM TO FAME	#46	MADEMOISELLE JESSICA

Sweet Valley Twins Super Editions

#1	THE CLASS TRIP	#6	THE TWINS TAKE PARIS
#2	HOLIDAY MISCHIEF	#7	JESSICA'S ANIMAL INSTINCTS
#3	THE BIG CAMP SECRET	#8	JESSICA'S FIRST KISS
#4	THE UNICORNS GO HAWAIIAN	#9	THE TWINS GO TO COLLEGE
#5	LILA'S SECRET VALENTINE		

Sweet Valley Twins Super Chiller Editions

#1	THE CHRISTMAS GHOST	#6	THE CURSE OF THE GOLDEN HEART
#2	THE GHOST IN THE GRAVEYARD	#7	THE HAUNTED BURIAL GROUND
#3	THE CARNIVAL GHOST	#8	THE SECRET OF THE MAGIC PEN
#4	THE GHOST IN THE BELL TOWER	#9	EVIL ELIZABETH
#5	THE CURSE OF THE RUBY NECKLACE		

Sweet Valley Twins Magna Editions

| THE MAGIC CHRISTMAS | | A CHRISTMAS WITHOUT ELIZABETH |
| BIG FOR CHRISTMAS | | #100 IF I DIE BEFORE I WAKE |

#47 JESSICA'S NEW LOOK
#48 MANDY MILLER FIGHTS BACK
#49 THE TWINS' LITTLE SISTER
#50 JESSICA AND THE SECRET STAR
#51 ELIZABETH THE IMPOSSIBLE
#52 BOOSTER BOYCOTT
#53 THE SLIME THAT ATE SWEET VALLEY
#54 THE BIG PARTY WEEKEND
#55 BROOKE AND HER ROCK-STAR MOM
#56 THE WAKEFIELDS STRIKE IT RICH
#57 BIG BROTHER'S IN LOVE!
#58 ELIZABETH AND THE ORPHANS
#59 BARNYARD BATTLE
#60 CIAO, SWEET VALLEY!
#61 JESSICA THE NERD
#62 SARAH'S DAD AND SOPHIA'S MOM
#63 POOR LILA!
#64 THE CHARM SCHOOL MYSTERY
#65 PATTY'S LAST DANCE
#66 THE GREAT BOYFRIEND SWITCH
#67 JESSICA THE THIEF
#68 THE MIDDLE SCHOOL GETS MARRIED
#69 WON'T SOMEONE HELP ANNA?
#70 PSYCHIC SISTERS
#71 JESSICA SAVES THE TREES
#72 THE LOVE POTION
#73 LILA'S MUSIC VIDEO
#74 ELIZABETH THE HERO
#75 JESSICA AND THE EARTHQUAKE
#76 YOURS FOR A DAY
#77 TODD RUNS AWAY
#78 STEVEN THE ZOMBIE

#79 JESSICA'S BLIND DATE
#80 THE GOSSIP WAR
#81 ROBBERY AT THE MALL
#82 STEVEN'S ENEMY
#83 AMY'S SECRET SISTER
#84 ROMEO AND 2 JULIETS
#85 ELIZABETH THE SEVENTH-GRADER
#86 IT CAN'T HAPPEN HERE
#87 THE MOTHER-DAUGHTER SWITCH
#88 STEVEN GETS EVEN
#89 JESSICA'S COOKIE DISASTER
#90 THE COUSIN WAR
#91 DEADLY VOYAGE
#92 ESCAPE FROM TERROR ISLAND
#93 THE INCREDIBLE MADAME JESSICA
#94 DON'T TALK TO BRIAN
#95 THE BATTLE OF THE CHEERLEADERS
#96 ELIZABETH THE SPY
#97 TOO SCARED TO SLEEP
#98 THE BEAST IS WATCHING YOU
#99 THE BEAST MUST DIE
#100 IF I DIE BEFORE I WAKE (MAGNA)
#101 TWINS IN LOVE
#102 THE MYSTERIOUS DR. Q
#103 ELIZABETH SOLVES IT ALL
#104 BIG BROTHER'S IN LOVE AGAIN
#105 JESSICA'S LUCKY MILLIONS
#106 BREAKFAST OF ENEMIES
#107 THE TWINS HIT HOLLYWOOD
#108 CAMMI'S CRUSH
#109 DON'T GO IN THE BASEMENT
#110 PUMPKIN FEVER
#111 SISTERS AT WAR

SIGN UP FOR THE SWEET VALLEY HIGH® FAN CLUB!

Hey, girls! Get all the gossip on Sweet
Valley High's® most popular teenagers
when you join our fantastic Fan Club!
As a member, you'll get all of this really
cool stuff:

- Membership Card with your own
  personal Fan Club ID number
- A Sweet Valley High® Secret
  Treasure Box
- Sweet Valley High® Stationery
- Official Fan Club Pencil (for secret
  note writing!)
- Three Bookmarks
- A "Members Only" Door Hanger
- Two Skeins of J. & P. Coats® Embroidery
  Floss with flower barrette instruction
  leaflet
- Two editions of *The Oracle* newsletter
- Plus exclusive Sweet Valley High®
  product offers, special savings,
  contests, and much more!

Be the first to find out what Jessica & Elizabeth Wakefield are up to by joining the
Sweet Valley High® Fan Club for the one-year membership fee of only $6.25 each
for U.S. residents, $8.25 for Canadian residents (U.S. currency). Includes shipping
& handling.

Send a check or money order (do not send cash) made payable to "Sweet Valley
High® Fan Club" along with this form to:

SWEET VALLEY HIGH® FAN CLUB, BOX 3919-B, SCHAUMBURG, IL 60168-3919

NAME _____
(Please print clearly)

ADDRESS _____

CITY_____ STATE _____ ZIP_____
(Required)

AGE _____ BIRTHDAY_____ /_____ /_____

Offer good while supplies last. Allow 6-8 weeks after check clearance for delivery. Addresses without ZIP
codes cannot be honored. Offer good in USA & Canada only. Void where prohibited by law.
©1993 by Francine Pascal   LCI-1383-123